Other books by Sherrie DeMorrow:

Knight and Daye
Cloud of Dreams
The Elder Rose
All The Land
The Little Bird
Beyond the Land
A Little Princess
Romancing the West

ROMANCING THE WEST

BY

SHERRIE DEMORROW

Published 2019 by

Lightning Source (UK) Ltd
Chapter House,
Pitfield,
Kiln Farm,
Milton Keynes
MK11 3LW,
UK

Cover Art Design by Sam Wall

To LL for help and support

In acknowledgment of JF, AA, and DB

and

To the Memories of RF, SH, CO'C, KC, LLG, LB,
and especially TO'C, who inspired this story

PREFACE

Although this could not be mentioned before, please be advised that there are sections of this book, as in the previous books, that contain *actual* life experiences, emotions and memories. In the guise of fiction, it is the only way to inform the public of the results of an extreme lifestyle and treatment toward a helpless child (now fully grown and *still suffering daily, the aftershocks of such treatment*). It is to be further noted that this individual suffers from a spectrum disorder called Asperger's Syndrome, which is a form of Autism. The author hopes this will not affect the enjoyment of the following, as well as the previous stories already written.

Despite the disclaimer in the aforementioned paragraph, please note this is still a book of fiction. The reader must suspend all preconceptions of belief in past history, as this book is not meant as an accurate representation of historical events (except in the case described in previous paragraph).

The historical attitudes towards sensitive issues, and people's prejudices of the time, had to remain intact to provide a sense of realism in the story. Nothing represented herein had been harmed during the writing of this work. Any personalities referred to herein are used solely in loving tribute to them.

Some place names given are **NOT** real, unless otherwise stated or recognised as real (or based on real places). The characters (for the most part) are fictional and loosely based on people known of by the author.

PART I – TIMOTHY AMBROSSI DAYE (EARLY TO MID-1800S)

CHAPTER I

The sun alighted high in the sacred heart of the bleeding West, a vast panorama of territory and teepees; its colour was auburn new, being early in the morning. The surrounding rocks bounced a rufescent glow on the far-reaching plains of the territory that reached out, and overwhelmed the natural order of things... like thunder in the sky. People back East had plunged their lives, wives and livelihoods, like one's cherry-ripe member, right into the land where they wanted to settle. They took their wagon trains and railèd pains, with all the hopes and dreams of an extraordinary race, determined to be the first ones *out there...*

... risking it all...

... and not giving a fig about the Natives upon the land.

And my folks were no different from them; in fact, they made it *out there* in the decades or so following the War of 1812. My family travelled from the Eastern shores, landing in New York, aboard a packet from Southern Ireland, full of people who packed themselves in suitcases to be taken across the sea. Their family came from a very small region of County Cork called Oconnalow, a name fusing two lovers from deep in the Irish mists of time.

Quite recently though, news filtered down about a famine that had driven much of our countrymen away, into the New World of the United States...

Where a better future awaited them
Or so they thought...
But as those newcomers crept into the Easternmost territories,
Their own hopes rested on a fistful of Sundays.
Those Sundays were packed with counter-wit,
And they were welcomed by the settled residents
Like talcum powder sprinkled upon dark fabric...

... for that was how we were perceived, and the concept of work could not accompany a garland's breath of fresh air.

They struggled.

We struggled, too...

... during those early times we remained in New York.

Yet, Pa would not be confounded, and persisted in his conquering mission of self-betterment... to work and make good for his family, which was just Ma at the time...

... when they tried to expand, the first attempt did not survive. Circumstances could not share itself with a baby, so they put this off for awhile.

Lucky for my folks, Pa landed a job as a labourer, working with a chandler. He worked long hours, feeding the masses with light; he set part of his wages aside for the long term, which accumulated nicely in a local bank. Once he made enough to leave New York, he upped sticks, took his dear Emmathy, and left the heated exhaust of that bustling City.

There was no love lost between him and those in the City; he didn't like them nor they, him. He spat on the rug of the rich, who were in charge, and thought to himself, *I'm gonna make it.*

One day, he followed in the footsteps of other waggoners who decided to change their destiny...

... and headed Westward...

... going the slow, painstaking way...

... a way that made them and their egos, and forged hope into their restless spirits.

They shared with other people and took turns helping one another out, steering their horses toward new lives...

... until...

A group of Indians woke up on the wrong side of their teepees, resolving to wage their mini-conflicts upon travellers encroaching on *their* territory...

(... in other words, they'd decided to burn in their Native delight and melt in agonising formation.)

So, they took action against the settlers, who were pretty well armed themselves...

... but those weapons could not compare to the trusty tomahawk...

... that had its day within the scalps of Man...

... the White Man, that is...

Thankfully, my folks were spared (*one cannot guess why*), for the Indians needed hands to carry the newly acquired supplies back to their encampment...

... then, they were held hostage by the tribe therein.

For a spell, they sat, wondering what to do. Ma and Pa never encountered this shit before, and, thinking about some things being said about how rough life was *out there*, they had to live by their wits...

... and try to remember those fistful of Sundays back East.

Pa soon got hold of a gun, purloined from the supplies the Indians took away from the late settlers (*which was Pa's to begin with, duh!*). A warm-less chill went through Ma's body, as she watched her husband do a turn against the hurtful, hateful prairies of the Earth. Mass murder topped Pa's list, like a cherry on an ice-cream cake. The Natives couldn't stand a chance, losing to Pa's gun, defeated like a butchered animal. Emmathy tried to help him, but he would not allow this. *Guns and women don't mix*, he felt, and so, left Ma to do what she could...

... if anything at all.

Once Pa's angry streak catapulted to its conclusion, he rightly claimed the supplies and a wagon, continuing his intended mission...

... to go West.

* * * * * *

Meanwhile, during the endless travel, and the secure feeling my folks felt in their minds and souls, they begun relations. Soon, Ma fell out with me and Pa was obliged to look after her. In the slow going of it all, they had gone out as far as the city of Chicago, where they remained for some time…

Pa rented a room above the tavern, *The Hornèd Headdress*, and he got a job there too (*convenient!*). He worked nightly, while Ma stayed upstairs, waiting for him to return, and the inevitable birth...

The day arrived, in that steamy, South side of Chicago summer day of 1827, when I had made my way into the world...

... and there, I was born Timothy Ambrossi Daye, nicknamed Amber (for some reason), the son of Timmodem Ambrose Daye and Emmathy Daye...

... none the worse for wear, mind you.

My middle name reflected a female Italian forebear, who married into the Daye family, many centuries ago. The young lady was very dynamic and her mind shrieked like a desert sun... sort of like where we were, here. She was a poet (at some level), and attracted the charms of Timoseph Daye, who travelled to Italy to study art...

(...but enough about the history, that could be told later.)

Another Daye arose, thus, so Pa worked harder than ever before, knowing responsibility, but the titillating pull of hard whisky tempted him *too* much...

... then, he started drinking.

It had been a little at first, just to keep his late nights secure, or at least awake at the bar, as I suckled sweetly on Ma's chest.

Once I became of a stronger age, with a rugged streak, Pa decided to up-sticks again, after saving some more money, despite his spending on drink. He resumed his Westward project, and soon, we finally left Chicago...

...and made ready for a lifetime's worth of adventure.

* * * * * *

The beige-coloured Plains sprawled out around us, as I glimpsed out of the corner of my swaddling clothes. I saw hope and promise in those hills...

... preferably without Indian raids, of course.

When we did come up upon them, Pa showed hesitation and mistrust. Ma and I were ambivalent, as it could go either way. My young mind was undeveloped of the swift ways of the world, so an opinion, on my part, could not be formed...

... however, I would have to... *fast.*

The Indians did not cause us much trouble, after seeing me. Maybe they respected the young, no matter what its persuasion? This did not phase them, and we were made welcome along the way, through Native hospitality. *Perhaps I was special?*

Pa also knew guns and tots did not mix either, so, we used much of the supplies, and did a little trading for their trouble and for putting up with us. Tribal attitudes were different from place to place, and we did try to respect their ways, despite us wishing to live on *their* land. Everyone gave me entertaining consideration and Pa showed some pride when glancing at the young son that was me.

The journey felt infinite, as wild creatures, above and below, astounded us. Their nocturnal noises drowned out the cacophony of snores coming from Pa's nasal passages.

I grew up hard and grew up quick, as I took it all in my stride. I even helped out, if it made things easier, though little hands promoted a touch of clumsiness on my part.

During all this was the backdrop of my childhood, consisting of travel, wild animals, and wild Natives (whether they raided or not). These prairies took no prisoners and I certainly was *not* going to become one. We lived rough, using what we had and going into another town to find more work; this was the constant motion of our newfound lives. We felt like nomads, like the tribes of old. We went as far as the map's end and eventually found a suitable home called the Carsonage, so-named after the fellow (an old man called Al Carson) from whom they bought the property and parcel of land.

However, home life wasn't as rosy as it was thought to be...

Pa got drunk as a paw on an anthill; Ma, in absence of her stronger half, turned her affections upon *me*. So much so, I became a darkened sheep, in the blackest of night. I hated her, but for the love of a stronger word. My younger years became a den of iniquity within the salacial palace I called home. My mind became a raging furnace I called hell...

... then, the years took their toll, taking time to make their passage...

... and I soon became a man...

... a lean man...

... a strong man...

... and a man to be reckoned with.

My life opened its path before me.

CHAPTER II

Years passed, and I moved on from my folks, both having since died. I settled in a place called Anthorn and carried out my existence as a ranch hand...

... but my labours took their toll on me, and I went to see a local, Dr Holkeye Swaid.

I complained of aches and pains and enquired of such to him.

The doctor remarked snidely, 'Been drinking again, Daye? I know of your father.'

'I ain't nothin' like my father,' I moaned, my light tipples being nobody's business.

'Take your shirt off,' Swaid said, 'Let me check you.'

I did so, as an instrument was put over my chest and back area. He moved it around so suddenly, it tickled against the thick hair of my chest. My heart beat in speedy succession, which rivalled the Western railroad.

'You've got a fast heart rate. You should take it easy,' was the doctor's hasty conclusion.

'What about the aches and pains?'

'You work, don't you? Duh!'

'Yes, doctor, very hard, thank you.'

'Yeah, well don't overdo it. How long do you work for?'

'I put in about 10-12 hours a day,' I replied.

'Might want to cut back, or the cut will bite,' Swaid quipped, 'You married or with a girl?'

'No, to both,' I sighed, wishing it were otherwise.

'Perhaps that is your problem. Overwork, too much booze, no woman. What a life!'

'You could use a woman's touch very badly,' I stood up, putting my shirt back on, 'Right across your face.'

'Sorry, I didn't mean to poke at ya, but I think if you changed your life a bit, your body might make you more comfortable.'

'Yeah, and a woman,' I retorted back, paying his fee.

I fiddled with my necktie, restoring it to its proper place atop.

'It was good to see you again, Daye. I hope not to see you again too soon.'

'Thanks,' I called, walking out.

I stood in the main street of Anthorn, right in the middle of the prairies. What state it was, was anyone's guess, for the mapmakers hadn't been hired yet to ordinate this Godforsaken place.

It lay there... just there...

... and while this was going on, my life would take an alternate turn with the unusual person that was Cynthia.

She was adopted by maternal grandparents of a family whose name sounds like Growling Sky. Her natural father carried the illustrious name of Silardicus, that dated all the way back to ancient Rome. Her natural mother, unfortunately, was part of the family of the Growling Sky, and died shortly after Cynthia's birth. The father, Silardicus, had been unable to look after his young daughter and was aggressively driven away by the mother's parents (but not without giving her a baptism first at a local church, which was *his* duty as a Catholic). These maternal grandparents of Cynthia's came from a Germanic background of non-Christian heathenness, whose religion tore apart at the souls of man. *At least, Cynthia thought so...*

... and wondered if it was a front to disguise a greater falsehood.

She further felt that her grandparents, and those like them, were like destructive soil planted in the bountiful heart of America. They had taken over her life in a most cruel manner, but felt they did right by her...

... but she didn't think so.

They lived in the district of New York, where those of many origins congregated. *It was also a good place to hide a deep secret as well,* as Cynthia suspected her grandparents doing. Yet, it was where Cynthia lacked a sense of being in life. She was exposed to many things, but forbidden to partake in any of them that disagreed with the ways of her grandparents.

They went as far as an adoption to secure *total* control over her, and forced her to comply with their unyielding, demoralising, non-Christian, religious lifestyle. She felt like an odd fish, cooped up in a bowl she didn't belong in.

She spent so much time to please them, never to their satisfaction and she did not have the confidence to feel she was good enough for anything or anyone...

... and she was declared unworthy by others...

The grandparents never left anything alone and chastised the poor lass into the bedroom, where she stayed for hours on end...

... hating, goaded, jaded...

... so much so that it gave way enough to bring about an unsettled reality.

It was a most stifling existence, and the older Cynthia got, the more desperate she was becoming to discharge herself from those Growling Skies. She was raised with antiquity at her disposal and ideas that went out with the dinosaurs; whereas *her* idealism was fresh and youthful; *she was determined to make a life of her own*, for ill or good, and no one will distract her from this goal.

So, one day, she saw fit to become a runaway...

... and run away to a new self...

... somewhere...

... any ol' where...

... where Growling Skies did not exist.

She did accept some help from others on her travels, whether it be a crumb of sustenance or a full-out meal, a ticket toward that new destiny she was yearning for in dreams, or in happy and protective companionship. One person recommended the mission nearby, but as Cynthia was raised different, she felt uncertain to go into this Christian territory. Curiosity about her father, his religion, and whether she was part of it, would later arouse her, yet the questioning was left aside for now.

She was frightened, and, with an unspent ticket, made her way out of the rotting apple of her life to head West, just like everyone else had done and was doing at that time.

How far did that train take her? She did not care... as long as it was away from *them*...

... and then she entered the comforting bleakness ahead.

She got off the train many hours later, and ended up in the middle of Anthorn, a place where the littlest beings had big horns. This appealed to Cynthia and she decided to settle here. At the time, she was nervous about the surrounding mission, although there was curiosity in the air about it, especially now that she was far removed from the Growling Sky. The best chance for her was to carry onward, as she did so, bravely and slowly.

There was an Indian encampment nearby, whose tribe lent its name to the town, and Cynthia decided to take the chance with them. They were certainly different from what she was used to, but it seemed less offensive to her to partake in, compared to what she *really* wanted (but too scared to ask). The Indians took kindly on her, and noted her loner status. She explained her situation to their leader, Chief Whithog, who spoke perfect English...

... and educated long ago by a passing Catholic missionary, who passed away during a skirmish with another tribe.

He was sympathetic, as he saw her running away from white society and felt flattered that she was willing to take up the noble mantle of Indian culture and life. So, with a sense of Christian duty and use of good spoken English, Whithog allowed her to remain with the tribe indefinitely. They shared dreams, hopes, petty ideals and the one thing she needed...

... *love*... which she never got properly from anyone...

... but it was not like *that* kind of love.

The Chief even renamed Cynthia of the Growling Sky. He decided on the name Cindihan, after an Irish legend of Cinder Hands (about a young woman whose hands were badly damaged), told by one of the local missionaries. The name was appropriate too, as the kindly Indian spotted a more recent similarity inflicted on his new charge.

Whithog saw that Cynthia Cindihan, now called Cindy, had all the necessities of life, such as food, clothing, and shelter. The difference here was that she had to do it all on her own, with some help from the women. Cindy learned to put up her own teepee, hunt, skin and cook her own foodstuffs; as well as make clothing, while wearing second-hand ones that some of the women gave to her in the meantime.

Cindy lived well at the Indian encampment at Anthorn. The restrictive Eastern mannerisms faded away, and she felt she could express herself like everybody else, without reproach. Her speech, as intelligent as it was, slipped into a more colloquial dialect, quite different from how she had been raised to speak. No one minded that, either.

No one chased her down (for now), and no one asked her any questions about her former life. Everyone accepted Cindy and she returned the favour.

It would be foolish not to...

And, it was a good cover for Cindy, as she was protected from those Growling Skies of the East, (which she thought nothing but contempt for) and hid away as an Indian maiden...

... but oddly enough, never taken advantage of physically, due to Whithog's tribal custom of *keeping the genes to oneself.*

'You ain't one of us,' Whithog would say to her...

... but he allowed her to become one with the tribe in daily routines...

... housekeeping...

... and the instinct for the sacred hunt (though she hated killing animals)...

... yet, loved for her endless tolerance toward the Natives in the first place, which they never encountered.

'No one likes us, cos we're Indians,' was the Chief's answer to that.

Cindy was comfortable with them, after all, they gave her haven and respect, which she gave in return...

... when the Growling Skies of New York did not...

(... especially now that her grandparents reported her as a runaway.)

* * * * * *

One day, on her round of gathering water and a bit of wood (for the evening fires), did my path cross with this most illustrious miss...

... as I was on my way back to the ranch, after breaking in a horse.

She was short, with golden-highlighted auburn hair (tied at the back, sporting a fringe), a simple, Indian dress, and flimsy shoes. Her looks and the clothing seemed out of place, and I got interested. I had no one and I remembered Dr Swaid's advice about women. She was a pretty thing, and white, but wondered if the mismatched appearance suggested adoption by the local tribesman? There were cases of them, rolling around these parts. The adult mortality rate out here was extreme, and you did not know where you'd be heading for...

... unless you had your wits about you...

... or a handy case of that Eastern fistful of Sundays.

I wanted to approach. I looked up into the daytime clear... no passing ships... *darn.* The noise was just an eagle passing by, and it was a rather private area.

I pulled up my trousers and gun holster and walked my horse and self over to the girl...

... with gulped down pride.

'Howdy,' I greeted in a friendly tone.

She looked up... *what a man!*

'Hi,' she replied, drawing more water from the river beside her.

'Need help, missy?'

'Sure do. Y'all can help by carrying this up to the camp out yonder.' She pointed to the tribal dwelling.

'You live with them?'

'Yes, sir. I sure do,' she stated proudly.

Now, who was the one with the most pride?

'What's your name, little lady?'

'Cynthia. Cynthia Cindihan. You may call me Cindy. I'm from back East. I ran away from horrible grandparents.' She gave me a huge, cat-like grin, showing all that pride in her heart.

'I'm Timothy Ambrossi Daye, but do call me Amber. I was born in Chicago. I have no folks to run away from,' I smiled back.

From the Eastern sun of sin, to a traumatised Western bin, I pondered, thinking about my early struggles and curious about hers, but left it alone.

'Amber,' she repeated, as if in a trance. 'That's a mighty fine name y'got there.'

I blushed a thank you and walked alongside her, carrying a newly-filled water jug. We barely touched any wood together...

... my heart, though, thought of something else to touch.

She went off toward a brush and gathered some good solid sticks for the fires. I still held that water jug.

I fixed the sticks-in-a-sack to the horse's saddle and she got up to ride.

Lucky girl!

We made it back to the camp, when Whithog approached.

'Why thank you for assisting the young Cindy here. I see you've got the wood stuffs too.'

'Yep,' she said, putting the wood in a container. 'Amber helped me and I got to ride on his horse, too.'

Whithog approved... heartily. 'Y'did, did ya now? Well, why don't I invite Amber here for dinner? Would you like that? We've got all sorts... ya like venison?'

My mouth watered, as I could not resist a home-cooked meal, even if made by Indians. 'Sure, I'll stay. I'll get to know your young missy, too.'

Whithog noticed my remark and saw that I could not resist a beautiful woman, either. 'You've got eyes for that pretty maid, yeah? Watch it, boy, she's a tough one, if you decide to take a tumble with her.'

'I can handle a good tumble with anyone,' I boasted, staring at Cindy...

... *yummy*, I thought, as my mind raced down a plug hole.

'You can wash yourself up nearby, you found the lake near here; you take Cindy with you.'

'My pleasure,' I cooed.

'Awh, and I wanted to help with dinner,' Cindy protested.

He went up to her. 'Don't fester up my matchmaking attempt on ya. Here's a fine white fellow, you know, your kind of fellow. Word's out you're wanted back East. We've protect you this far, from those crazy lawmen. So do what I say and go with this hot potato of a man; you'll never reach the famine stage with him. Now, you go out and enjoy y'self, y'hear?'

She stared at Whithog... brown eyes to brown eyes. 'Okay, I'll do it... for you.'

'Not for me, but for you. We've enough women to help feed the county; so you best be gettin' movin' and clean up.'

'Yes sir,' she cast herself down into submission...

... but this time, it was a *willing* submission...

... the time when we cleaned up together was something to reckon with.

CHAPTER III

We returned to the river where I'd met Cindy earlier.

'You take your clothes off now, and clean up real good,' she ordered, as a dare for me.

'You turn 'round, missy... go on,' I circled my finger to give her the hint.

'And deprive me of a natural wondrous beauty, no sirree!'

'I know you've been around, my dear,' I began to creep toward her, ' And this time, you'd gone too far.'

I made a grab for her, clothes and all, and threw her into the river.

What a surprise she got!

I giggled wildly, not noticing that she'd jump out and catch me from behind. She wrestled with me and attempted to strip me bare.

She was successful atop; the bottom, well...

'Now now, you little she-cat,' I panted, removing my belt, 'I'll do this bit.'

'That ain't good 'nough,' she hissed.

I grinned and told her to step aside...

... and went to the river to remove my trousers beneath the secluded water...

... but it weren't the *biting* fish I was worried about...

'How modest can y'get,' she yelled out. 'I thought it was us womenfolk behind the rude screens!'

'Sorry darling,' I winked devilishly, tossing my wet apparel aside on the bank. I then beckoned her, 'Now come and get me, if you want me.'

I could tell she liked a fine do-or-dare situation and I gave her a good one. It was alluring, titillating and, on my part, sexy...

... which was what I was trying to do to hook her up to me...

... and potentially save her from the Territory's finest.

Cindy went behind a tree and removed her throw-on Indian dress, emerging from *her* rude screen, and clutching it in modesty.

'Come on in, honey,' I wooed, with the largest *come-on* this virgin territory hadn't seen for a long time, if at all...

... assuming the Indians had similar wooing practises.

Putting the beaded fabric gently aside my saturated gear, she joined me...

... it was love at first sight...

... and a sight of real radiance.

I knew there was someone hiding under that tough-shit-Sherlock veneer of hers.

'I like y'all. You're very pretty for a man,' she firmly announced, fingering the thick bustle of hair on my chest.

'If I'm pretty, then you must be luxuriating in splendour,' my voice intoned smoothly in return.

'Just don't luxuriate your splendour in the grass or you'll run into them cowpats, y'know.'

She had a fantastic way of romancing the goal.

I sniggered at her joke, and splashed that untamed beast before me.

'I'll handcuff you before y'even try, sir!'

'I'll raid your home and make crude love in the passion of your bedroom, surrounding you so, you cannot touch the ceiling.'

'Nyahh,' she taunted at my seductive remark.

I nyahhed back at her with another splash.

'Ahhh,' she cried, grabbing at my middle section, tickling me.

I fell over backwards with a bigger splash upon her, then jerked straight up, looking at the sky. The moon started its opaque appearance and the sun descended on the other side.

'We better get going,' I said, as I parted myself from the water, leaving Cindy in her cindered dampness. I began to dress, as wet as my clothes were. The Natives might provide something more temporary, while they dried...

... I hoped.

'Hey, wait for me,' she panicked and ran toward me.

She left her nakedness behind, and now clad in her Indian finery (well, as close to finery as she could get).

'You can pass for one of them,' I complimented.

'You'd pass for a cowpoke,' she retorted, giggling.

'Come here,' I held her and we melted into each other, then and there, with the lusciousness of nature around us.

The kissing was phenomenal and she handled me like a pro...

... *a pro what,* I could not imagine...

... but it made me think about other men she'd probably met over the years...

... *if she did.*

As if to read my mind, she duly answered, 'Y'all don't have to worry about other men folk. I like you... I'm crazy about you.'

Oh really?

I stared back at her. 'Yeah?'

She nodded with conviction.

'Yessum. I dig your pony-scratching ways and your endless mess about the haze.'

Good Lord, what a pick-up line...

... and I've struck a mine...

... not a gold mine, see, but something more precious than gold...

... *at least the highlights in her hair were golden.*

We walked back to the Native camp, where we had a lovely dinner made by several of their womenfolk, excluding Cindy...

... *cos that sweet little ol' princess was with me!*

The food was of varied meats, mostly game animals, corn, and bread. They made home brews from local plants, corn, and grapes (though I doubt they all went into the same pot).

Whithog paused from his endless joyous consumption to ask me, 'You two got acquainted?'

I looked at Cindy and back at him. 'I think we had, yes.'

'Good. I can see by your clothing that you had a willy of a time in that yon river,' he smirked.

So much for the dried-clothes theory... *was I that obvious?* I guess no one could pull wool over the fellow.

'Okay, we had time together yes...'

Suddenly I had an idea...

... and a proposal to make...

'Sir, I know you were caring for Cindy all the while and I was wondering if I could take her off your hands. What do you think?'

Whithog was astounded by my comment. 'What do I think? What do I think?'

He paused...

... enough to hear one's heart beating...

... *rapidly...*

'I think you're nuts to take on such a woman. But I will not stop you. Miss Cindihan here had been a fine addition to the tribe and we all enjoyed her contributions to our society. However, us men folk here don't wish to marry her, umm... cos she's white and all and we don't like to bleach our genes now... no offence to your kind.'

'None taken.' I rolled my eyes at his lurid joke.

'I will let you marry the girl, if that pleases you,' Whithog offered.

Marriage, me? God, this was sudden. I only just got to know her, the she-cat that she was.

'Y'don't have to answer this here second,' the Chief continued. 'You get some sleep and think it over. I suggest you both bunk up, to see if living with her is worth the hassle.'

Cindy laughed heartily and said, 'I can make room for one more in my tent any day.'

'I bet you could,' I sneered at her.

'Well, she's your kind, your blood, y'all keep together,' Whithog concluded.

This will be a night that promised not to pass us by. I put my arm around her and kissed her, not giving a price as to what he thought of it...

... and I noticed he would use a good wide-screen sized rude screen to hide his own behind, I smirked to myself.

We spent the next few hours talking, gallivanting and keeping the fires burning 'til bedtime.

It was a night I slept so peacefully, even the native animal calls didn't give me a stitch.

CHAPTER IV

The next several weeks, I retained my labour. It weren't so bad; it brought in good money for me...

... but my mind was fixed on a stubborn bull of another kind... *Cindihan*.

Although she wasn't really a bull (more like a heifer, to me), her temperament could rob one of its own dignity.

One Sheriff Martin had been led to the Indian encampment where Cindy was staying. However, Whithog would have none of that *white-man-trash business*, as he called it, and sent her out on an errand with one of his men. *He knew there would be no ramblin' between them.*

The Sheriff rode into the encampment and dismounted. He had a quick and quiet look around, before he walked over to him, horse reins in his hand.

He said gravely, 'You big boss here?'

Whithog faced him, his regalia showing off his leadership status. 'What do you think? I'm Chief Whithog, at your service.'

'We believe there is a young lady, a runaway, going by the name of Cynthia of the Growling Sky, passing through the area, or living nearby. Had you seen her?'

'Now why would I get involved in the affairs of some white girl, unless we has her hostage... and we do not take hostages! We don't believe in that sort of thing. We live in peace, unless someone wants a piece of us and I don't think a little sissy girl you describing would have the balls to mess with us. Nah, she ain't here!'

Martin nodded, quite easily defeated. 'I see. Let us know if you see her.'

The Sheriff remounted the horse and left Whithog in the dust that was his home. Whithog was real good at getting other people's snouts out of his trough, but how long could he take preventative measures?

He sent word to me, passing the message through one of his warriors called Coltrane...

... because Whithog sensed trouble...

... and trouble was not where he wanted to be...

Coltrane rode through the Lorrainum Valley, crossing Torkhelson Bay, to find me with my mean stallion...

... well he wasn't *mean*, as such, just a bit jittery.

Coltrane called out to me, 'Amber, Amber, come quick.'

I didn't recognise him and held my hunches. 'Yeah, what is it?'

'Whithog needs you on the double. Your girl is wanted. The Sheriff come to camp a-searchin'.'

I made my break, mounted my horse, and rode out with Coltrane to see what the fuss was about...

... and it did not look good.

Whithog fetched Cindy, and once I arrived, we were brought before him.

'Amber Daye,' he said, 'We've a problem. A big problem...'

I waited on him in despair for her, though I knew it were not a judgment upon me.

'... The Sheriff had come looking for your little girl, causing disruption to our people in the camp. We don't want any trouble here, we like how we live, and we had, until you folk come crawling and sniffing 'round.'

'I understand,' I nodded.

Cindy got nervous and reached for my hand to hold...

... which did not go unnoticed by Whithog.

'Miss Cindihan,' he continued, 'I see you've driven for an affection toward Amber Daye.'

We looked at one another and we answered, 'Yes.'

He gave us an ultimatum. 'Well, had y'considered that marriage proposal I suggested to you earlier? It's either matrimony for you two, or a-gaggèd home for your girl. Got the point?'

I remembered that day I met her at the river and that evening meal we shared with Whithog and his tribe. I reflected further and decided to help the young lady out.

I asked, 'What's it she's wanted for?'

A nervous silence passed between us.

'Fella said something about her being a runaway. I didn't think folks get in trouble for running away,' Whithog replied. 'He just rode his big white butt onto my land and asked about her wherewithals, or something. Of course, I denied ever even knowing her; I sent her away, so she wasn't even here when the Sheriff came a-snoopin'. Cindy deserves better anyway. She's a good girl, under that hard-cased shell of hers. I'm too fond of her to give her up. A man like you could look after her better, and maybe even breed, if you know what I mean.'

He began to laugh, winking and nudging me at the side. Then he carried on, 'The Great Totem knows I, nor my men, could help her any further. She should be with her own kind, y'hear.'

'I hear ya,' I concurred. I then addressed the girl. 'It won't be easy, but it may be fun. I know I gotta get ya outta here, 'fore that Sheriff returns, *if* he does.'

Cynthia gave me a hug and said, 'I shall go to the end of this continent for you, and fall off, if need be.'

Whithog smiled. 'Good, then it's all settled. I can get someone from the mission to officiate your ceremony. They're just a few miles from here. I'll send out Coltrane for youse.'

I was more than chuffed at his offer. The Mission of St. Jacquet was only a few miles away, and had plenty of priests to help us. Cindy bit the bullet and enquired of a priest regarding her father's deed of baptising her. Word got back that the matter would be looked into.

'It's either that, or she goes back to her family, whom I figured weren't very civil to her,' Whithog glumly added.

I gave Cindy a kiss. 'It looks like we'll be seeing one another for a good long while.'

'I could not look into a better looking glass,' she swooned.

Coltrane gushed a geyser full of sentiment. 'Awh shucks, don't she have a way with words, them missies.'

'Let her save that for the bedroom,' he laughed, 'They can then both gush 'pon each other.'

The two Natives laughed their headdresses off, at our expense, but we didn't care. They were just teasing the sloppiness away.

* * * * * *

And so it came to pass, that Cynthia and I would be wed by the next full shining moon...

... which was only a few days away...

... so there ain't no turning back or nothing.

The earlier harassment of Sheriff Martin was put in check when the Warrior Coltrane put a socket in his stump and herded the cowpat outta the territory...

... but her mangy, nefarious grandparents, who retained the plea against her as a runaway, sought help further afield...

... spreading far and wide...

... and so, thought they knew best for her...

... but didn't.

They still wanted control over their charge, which presented a real threat to our wedding plans...

... it was either me or them...

... and I certainly knew who Cindy would choose.

I shall not escape from our potential wedded bliss, for I surely wanted it, and I, alone, would be in charge of the little lady... *not them.*

I shall get that dear woman to be mine...

... whether she liked it or not...

... and I believed she would.

We'd been getting quite amorous with one another, too...

... and oh, she'd been treatin' me good alright, I heaved with a sigh.

I couldn't wait to wed her...

... and when that day came, a man rode out from the Mission to officiate the match. He first went straight to Cindy and confirmed that by word of a priest from the church in New York, she had been baptised and that she was Christian all along, *despite what her grandparents did and said to her.*

Then later, the ceremony began.

The priest cited, after reading the preambles and whatnot in his book, 'Do you, Timothy Ambrossi Daye, take this woman to be your lawful wedded wife... 'til death do you part.'

'I do,' I stated firmly.

'Do you, Cynthia Cindihan, take this man to be your lawful wedded husband... 'til death do you part.'

'I do,' she answered.

I put an Indian-made ring on her finger.

The priest concluded, 'I now pronounce you man and wife.'

We then kissed... *proudly*. Recalling that I overheard her conversation with the priest, I thought to initiate her *my way*…

I grabbed a nearby bucket, filled it with water and doused her, good and proper with it…

... here's your baptism, sweety, and don't ya forget it; you're one of us now, for sure!

She squealed and chased me through the encampment, much to the delight of the other Indians.

After the initial congratulatory spell and feasting, the priest made out a certificate to prove our union, and Whithog sent his best wishes to us. 'Now that I've put you white folks together, You'd better be off with youse into the next town. Make a move and keep moving, 'til you fall off this here land.'

I knew what he meant... Cindy expressed a similar feeling. I shook his hand 'I appreciate your kindness toward us, and thank you for looking after her.'

'Well, don't get too attached here, it ain't nothing personal, see. Now you look after her, boy, and do a good job. I knows y'can,' Whithog said. 'I'll set you up with something to make your trip a little easier. You got a horse?'

'Yes,' I answered, 'My stallion.'

'I'll get you a cart to hitch him up to with some supplies.'

He either seemed too generous, or was he trying to get rid of us?

Once the thanks and honours were over, Cindy and I headed out into a very long wilderness...

... with more Indians to encounter and a virgin land to conquer...

... though the one virgin here was just fine.

After settling down a few miles away from Whithog's encampment, we pitched up for the night. I came over to her, 'Awh, Cindy, you my wife now. Sorry about that earlier soaking... do you have any regrets or reservations?'

'I've got none to live on, and there ain't nothing like a kick of reality to build your boot straps. Give me another kiss, Amber.'

We did just that...

... and I found her verbiage quite appealing.

Eventually, after a bit of fumbling and fondling, we did cross the state line with one another, unmarked as it was, like the great nation before us. We blended with virile gusto, when I spilled my wetness into her. I suddenly withdrew and cleaned up my spent, rotting filth onto a towel stationed nearby.

Cynthia looked at me as if I were crazy.

'Just making myself more presentable to you,' I explained.

'Y'don't have to do that. You my man now, I don't care what its says on the cup; I accept you as you are, sir.'

I hovered over her and poked her tummy. 'But it's what's inside that counts.'

'Well, if your inside's been spent, we'd have to go elsewhere to spend it again, don't we?'

Those atypical words of hers... *aughhh!*

'Why are you so damn poetic, my tough little one? Are you goin' soft on me? You drivin' me mad.'

'Good,' she smirked at me, 'I's a fixin' to drive you wild for me.'

I surprised her with my take on words. 'You'll need to get your tool-kit out, if you hadn't done so already.'

She threw a cushion at me, and I lunged at her, begging for another kiss. We looked into each other's eyes and we could both tell there was plenty of love between us.

I then asked her, 'What if your grandparents come scoutin' for ya?'

'They could scout all they want, don't mean they'll get any help by it. We crossed the state line, and you done made a woman outta me. I'm now a fully fledged woman, I am!'

So stated with such conviction.

CHAPTER V

We rode along the path to our destiny; after a few weeks of on-the-fly jobs and *roughing it*, we decided to indulge ourselves to a real honeymoon. The togetherness we shared was great, but not in the open prairies. I had some cash from the work and the supplies were dwindling. We ended up in the Biobay region, where we stopped for the night at a boarding house called *The Three Bells*. The house itself was located at a junction point, near a railroad line in the Cataloo Valley. It was a light green gabled house with white windows and black shutters. It had a countrified look, and homey feel to it, and this made it irresistible to many. I thought it would be ideal for us, and we went inside.

The place was done up well, with lace-lined cushions bordering elegant French styled sofas, framed pictures on the walls depicting rural Western scenes and the occasional portrait of a past president. The check-in desk was ordered and I approached it to ring the bell.

An averaged sized older man came out of the back room office, wearing round-eyed glasses and a crownless hat with a black front brim. He was dressed well, but modestly.

He greeted me. 'Bonjour, how may I help you today?'

I smiled nervously, my French being slightly below par. 'Bonjour to you. We'd like a room for the night, please.'

'One room or two,' the proprietor eyed us carefully.

'Preferably one, please. We are married.'

'Oh yeah?'

Cindy showed him her ring and I added, 'We were married by a priest from the mission of St Jacquet.'

Recognition appeared in his face. 'Ah oui, St Jacquet! I remember the Mission. You shall have the bridal suite. You on a honeymoon?'

'Ah, yeah, we are,' I looked at Cynthia and smiled.

My eye caught another picture on the wall... the famed Admiral Nelson. What the blazes was *he* doing here, out in this part of the New World?

'I could not help noticing your portrait of Nelson, Mr...,' I began.

'My name is Monsieur Nelsonne Du B'Guerre, but you can call me Monsieur Du, and my partner is Madam Emilie (Emma) Pique. She's working in the back. We're in business together.'

'I see. It is a fine memento.'

'Good icebreaker.' Cindy then rolled her eyes.

'You wonder why I have a picture of a British Admiral within my premises, yes? Well, I'll tell you. I was named after him, which is why I am called Nelsonne. My family sided with the king, during the Revolution of 1789. We were on the run from the Chopper-on the-Square for a long time. When I was born, they named me Nelsonne, out of spite toward the radicals. When the War was over, I had grown up, got married and settled...'

I caught a glimpse of his other half in business, as she strolled by.

He continued. '... anyway... some years later, the miserable people of Paris wanted to re-enact 1789 again and commenced *another* revolt. I took the old side and stood my ground. My wife died suddenly and we had no children between us. I was on the run, this time alone, just like many years before. I left France to make it in America. I met Madam Pique on the way there and found she had been widowed by that same revolt. So, you see, we have much in common and we decided to head West, as the port we landed in was overbearing to us. I know your country has no king, but there is no king like free enterprise, n'est ce pas?'

He gave a laugh and smiled greedily at me.

'Right,' I said in return, 'Now what about that room?'

'Ah, oui, monsieur, sorry.' Monsieur Du rustled through some papers and found the register for me to sign. He turned to a key press on the wall. Here you are, room number 12. It's spacious and there's an adjoining washroom.'

Like I needed a bath?! 'Oh?'

'There are two bathtubs, divided in the middle for modesty, along with a basin.'

'Well,' I smiled at Cindy, thinking of *my* kind of greed, 'Nothing but the best here.'

The elder man beamed, seeing my enthusiasm. 'Would you be dining with us? For an extra dollar, you can have dinner and breakfast in the morning.'

I could not resist the food offer. 'Done.'

'That will be five dollars altogether.'

I dug in my pocket and gave him the money.

'Merci. Enjoy your stay.'

I took the key and headed upstairs with my wife to that notable room of number 12. When I opened the door, I just flopped onto the ever-present double bed, which was dressed in a patchwork quilt with a stand on each side. A lamp was provided atop them, and a large wooden wardrobe loomed in its presence from the other side of the room.

I got up and walked into that adjoining washroom and was pleased to see those promised bathtubs back to back with a divider in between. It was just as the fellow said...

... and it also gave me an idea.

I went to tell Cindy. 'How would you like a good pampering, darling?'

'Me, pampered? No one ever did that for me. Why, what you got in mind?'

I motioned to her to come to see *that* room.

'Golly, ain't that something you see in them fancy homes back East?'

'This is the bridal suite.'

'*Two* bathtubs?'

''Tis the era, my dear. They're probably too small for two to use together, anyhow.'

'Practical minded you, eh? Let's go in.'

I turned on the taps to fill the baths. I also noticed a pile of soap bars. I read the packaging. *Bath Humbugs?*

I hadn't gotten out of my clothes yet, so I went down to the desk to enquire.

Madam Pique came out this time and said, 'Ah, we got them on the way here via England. We took a few with us and found them to be very handy. We now have a contract with the company that makes them and they send us their off-cuts, wrapped like their regulars. They are not on for show, you know. You may use them.'

I thanked her and went back upstairs to refresh myself. I got undressed and grabbed a nearby towel. I climbed hastily into the pleasant-feeling bathwater, the taps having done their job.

'Cindy, love, could you get me one of those soap things?'

She went up to the basin and picked up one.

'You mean these?'

'Duh... give it here!'

Out of curiosity, she read the packaging. '*Bath Humbugs of Fullonum. Made in Totteringstate, England. By Appointment to Her Maj--...*'

'Give me that,' I fussed, cutting her off.

'Okay, don't get so worked up, or your scales will fall off.'

'Isn't that what I'm in the bath for?'

She gave me the soap. Silly mistress now had me reading the fucking wrapping. *Made in Totteringstate, England.* Now, that was a funny name for a place. Fullonum was even funnier, but I didn't mind. *I could look that one up later.*

Totteringstate... had a nice ring to it.

I took the soap out of its illustrious wrapping. I called to my dearest to put the wrapping aside for another time... *maybe we could get some for ourselves one day.*

I began cleaning, using a scrubbing brush hanging in front of the tub.

I called out, 'When are youse coming in?'

She approached the doorway. 'You can close your eyes, Amber honey.'

'Oh no, we're married now. I made you a woman, you said so yourself.'

'I knows that. Modesty do run deep, you know.'

I gave her a splash. She removed her newly wet clothes and entered the *other* bath.

'Oooh, this here's nice. Thanks, Amber.'

'Don't mention it.'

I heard some frantic splashing about. 'Shit, I forgot the soap.'

'Here, use mine.'

I threw the item over the divider. It splooshed in front of her.

'Amber!'

I giggled and carried on scrubbing myself. *Was I so clean, now?* It was hard to tell. One could cleanse the body, tho' the soul and mind were a different breed of animal. I kept to myself and let the little lady get on with her lot. I was astonished at all the luxury surrounding me. Ma and Pa would never have succumbed to this sumptuous space, if they'd ever found it.

I got up and looked over the border between us. Cindy was still scrubbing away...

... I took a tin cup on the ledge and filled it. Then, I tipped its contents right over the side...

... and onto her head.

She screamed, 'Amber Daye!'

I sat down in my bath and giggled, caressing myself in the bathwater. I soon got up and wrapped the towel around my lower half.

I walked over to her side.

'So, how's your bath?'

She made a face at me. I teased her with a wicked smile.

Her response was tempting. 'If this here tub was big enough...'

'Well, it isn't and you can't.' I gave her a good nyahh and went in to get dressed.

'Amber?'

I leaned into the doorway, facing her.

'Come on here,' she beckoned.

I strode toward the tub...

... and she grabbed my towel and uncovered me.

'Oooh, you nag,' I cried, attempting to recover it.

She eyeballed me cruelly, as she lowered the nice, fluffy, dry, white towel into her bath.

'No, no, please,' I begged helplessly.

The tip of the towel was immersed, when her mind swiftly changed course (which was a woman's prerogative).

'Awh, alright. Here y'go. Ya big sissy.'

She threw the towel back and I hastily repaired myself and ran back to the room to get dressed quick, before she had any other naughty ideas.

CHAPTER VI

The next day, we set off into the star-suns toward the West. Into the breeze, we flowed hereon through our journey past...

... past rocks, moonstones and small animals of the wild sort...

... not unlike my dear wife, Cindy Daye.

We reached the Wyville Posting junction, where we had a rest and refreshment. Large troughs held well water for horses; we went in for a drink ourselves.

Cindy and I carried on afterwards, all saddled up in kit bags, wondering where we would spend the night. The area looked pretty eerie to me, and I did not like the way the grass was moving...

... *sssssssszzzz*...

... those weren't snoring bears, but hissing rattlers in the area.

I was un-amused at the newfound company, but Cindy didn't mind. When we got off the cart, she cocked her gun, ready to shoot at the motley beast that would *dare* to cross her path...

... however, it was her *mouth* that fired first.

'Amber!'

I quickly turned to face a beautifully brown coloured, black patterned and dangerous snake. This rat snake had eclipsed my vision of the Plains surrounding me.

'Sssssss,' it slurred at me, 'YYYe shall go no furtherrrrrr.'

'Oh yeah,' I smirked, 'And what if we do. How did you learn to talk like that and who gave you rights to this here territory anyway?'

'IIIIIIttthhhayyy,' it continued lisping verbal venom at me, 'IIIIIIssssssaaayyyy, what is willed be done.'

'Who are you, God? I don't think so,' I argued, 'You're a freak... a dangerous freak.'

'TTTTThhhhhhere are tttthhhoossssssse affftttther yyyyyyeeee,' the snake said, 'YYYYYeeeee aaaarrre being follllllllloweddd.'

'Wha-?' I stopped dead in my tracks. *Followed, by whom?* I thought we kicked that sheriff off our backs ages ago, and now that Cindy and I were married, no one could touch us.

'SSSSsssssshhhhe's sssstill a runaway, isssss sssssshe nnnnnooottttt?'

'But we're married,' I cried, 'No one could claim her now but ME!'

'TTTThhhhhere'ssssss nnnnooo sssssssense than tttttrrryyying,' the snake retorted.

'How the fuck would *you* know, anyway? You're a grisly animal, if I e'er saw one,' I snapped back.

'TTTTTaaakesssssss one to knowwwwww one, hhhhhuuuuuman,' it concluded.

'Awh, fuck you,' Cindy moaned, and pulled the trigger...

... but she was a crap shot and missed.

'YYYYYeeeeee cannnnnottttt kill meeeee,' the snake whispered, crawling around the horse's leg to disable it. 'Hhhheeeed my waaaarrrrnnnninnnng.'

'Oh no, oh no. Now you don't, you fu-,' I scrambled for my gun this time...

... now, it was my turn.

The gun aimed point blank at the snake...

... got it.

'YYYYYYeeeeee cannnot desssssstroy mmmmmeeeeee.... yyyyyyeeee cannnaaaa sssssssay I did not wwwwwaarrrrrrn yyyyyy-...'

The snake lay dead. I blew the residue smoke from the barrel and returned the gun to my holster, flicking it around my finger first.

I reflected upon what this biblically poetic snake had said to me, with regard to us being followed. It was either that or, heck, he was cheatin' at us.

I sat on the cart, Cindy took the seat next to me and we carried on the journey. I kept my eyes open; the dryness got to me though, and my state of mind was altered from talking to a freakin' snake. It was like witchcraft or something... *where did that fucker come from*, I wondered... *sheeesh!*

We rode on further when I decided to stop a moment.

Cindy asked, 'What about the snakes?'

'Don't worry about those damn serpents, child. They got nothin' on us. I shall protect you.'

She looked around nervously, still triggered in her lot, but took comfort in the words I said.

I opened my shirt a little and began to remove it. I didn't give a fiddle at the blazes of the light upon us, nor that I was in female company...

... for that was whom I wanted to arouse, as I was cooling off.

I slashed against a thorny pale bush and noticed a small stream nearby. I ran to it (still on my feet), once I'd finished and splashed myself, good and proper.

Cindy snuck up and pushed me in.

'Hey,' I gasped.

She laughed pretty heartily. 'Gotcha this time, dearest.'

I smiled and got up to give her a wide-eyed eyeful of me...

... to which she wished herself upon, clinging to me in desperation...

... then I tipped over.

We cooled off together vigorously, and dried ourselves in the climbing sun, nuzzling up cosy.

A small time had stretched and I felt we needed to get going. 'Let us continue. I feel better already.'

'Alright. Here's your shirt,' Cindy said.

'Keep hold of it for now.'

She shrugged her shoulders and returned to the horse and cart.

The sun reached its peak soon after and I was getting a bit hungry. I passed the idea to Cindy.

'I heard you could eat snakes, if you cook them right,' she suggested. 'You left one dead up yonder.'

'Well, I ain't a-goin' up yonder, am I? 'Sides, it's uncivilised to eat something you just spoke to. No thank you,' I spat at her idea.

My stubbornness went as far as it could, before giving way to the more heightened desire for food. My life repeated itself continually as we rode Westward, out in these distant lands. It was a big country, and you couldn't get to even know a fraction of it, if you tried. I looked around for signs of life and told her what I planned.

'Okay, but you'll have to go real wild.'

'We may be naked out here, my love, but we shall never be afraid... even if to kill. We'll lick this, you'll see.'

'I ain't lickin' that,' Cindy retorted.

I got off the cart and started exploring. There was plenty of life out here, and I began to load my gun.

'What're in the mood for, girl?'

Cindy looked at me. 'I'm easy. What ya got?'

'I'll have a look around. You gather some wood and grab a pot. I shall return.'

I gave her a kiss and went off to find... *something*.

After a bit of time having a good wander, I spotted a couple of jackrabbits doing their thing, ignoring all around them. As much as I hated to do it, I felt I had to get them both... one for me, one for her...

... so I hid behind a rock and prepared my gun. The rabbits sat together, resting or grooming, I didn't know. They tendered their needs, as I tendered mine...

... and aimed for both animals...

... *hey, it was either kill or go hungry*, and I was not one for starving.

I fired straight at the one, hoping for the shot, before they both ran for it...

... lucky for me, the one had caught the bullet.

I walked over to the fresh corpse...

… and found the other rabbit was shot clean through, too.

I guessed that rabbits weren't as fast as they boasted.

I took them by the ears and carried them over to Cindy, who started a roaring good fire. She got out the pot (from the supplies given to us by Whithog) and I prepared the meat. After the skinning and cutting up, we cooked ourselves a decent meal.

'Too bad these didn't come with vegetables,' she added.

'What do you think this is, four star dining with entertainment? Go eat some grass,' I suggested.

She looked around her. 'There's not enough.'

'Then tough turtles to you, ol' lady.'

She stuck her tongue out at me and got up to find something. She gathered whatever grass there was and added it to the meal.

I examined her finding. 'Is it poisonous?'

'You told me to eat the frickin' grass, y'all. So, here. Eat it.'

'Christ, I was just kidding you. I wouldn't do anything to threaten you, would I?'

'Nawh, I guess not. Dirty devil, you.'

I stuck my tongue at her this time.

'Awh, hush it Amber.'

I giggled and ate my part of the grass. She did as well and made a face.

I made a face too. 'My butt will pay.'

'We're not in a civilised place. Where's the next town?'

'How the hell should I know? It's not like I travelled these parts before,' I rasped.

She looked worried. 'We's fighting, aren't we?'

'Lord no, child. Come here.' I gave her a hug. 'Sorry I got wild on you. It's just the load of travelling. It makes me feel like a gypsy.'

'So, there's no one back home coming a-looking for me?'

'Why you ask? I do not believe so. We're too far out for those who were a-lookin' to make any commotion over ya.'

'You don't know my grandparents. They're…'

I tried to calm her. 'Shhhh, I wouldn't want to... look, we're married; don't you forget it.'

She looked at her ring. 'I won't. They'd suppressed me bad and made me feel sub-human, like as if I were an Indian or a slave. They live for control. Marriage to you won't stop them.'

'Ah, but the law will.'

'They'll bend and break it if they have to. They're good at that sort of thing.'

'I'll break their backs, if I have to, darling. Now stop frettin' and come close to me. You are mine, forever.'

I looked at her and gave her a kiss.

'As long as life gives us,' she answered back.

'Let it be for a long time... God, I love you,' I swooned in her arms.

We left the fires to burn off naturally, the food being consumed, bones thrown to the distant creatures beyond...

… and we slept in the middle of nowhere, *again*.

CHAPTER VII

Another several weeks of youthful journeying laid behind us, in our determined travel Westward. Living hand-in-pocket and ever-so-close together made our marriage rather challenging, but worthwhile. It showed us we could live with one another and that we made a good team. We were confident in our survival and took care of what we loved and owned (i.e., the horse, cart and little possessions we had). We co-mingled our goodness and I prayed earnestly that this goodness would flame within Cindy.

Soon, we headed toward a township of Antler Junction, near Agro Hill a northern district boarding with the territory of Nebraska. A train was set up nearby, but I decided to stick with the horse and cart for now.

Cindy moaned, 'God, I'm beat Amber. Could we stay here?'

'Yes we can. I still got a little something to spend, but we'll go easy this time. No frills, y'hear?'

'I hears ya.'

'Good.'

That settled it. I rode up the main street with buildings facing one another from the opposite side. I was surrounded by a touch of the civilised world, albeit a more *primitive* version.

I walked into Wandamont's General Store and perused its shelves. A bag of hard sugar candies had caught my fancy... *Aunt Esther's Suckas.*

The elderly black attendant came over to me. 'May I help you?'

'A bag full of Esther's please,' I said.

'Better than a bag full of Esther's face,' he quipped, thinking about the relative who made the candy. 'That'll be 60 cents, my good sir.'

I dug in my pocket and gave him the change.

'Thank you,' he replied.

I took the bag and went out to meet Cindy, who was waiting for me at the horse and cart.

'Whatcha got, Amber?'

'A bagful of candies. Want one?'

She held the bag and read the packaging instead... (*what was with her and packaging?*) *'Aunt Esther's Suckas, Guaranteed a Mouthful of...'*

'Give me that,' I grabbed the bag and dove into it. 'Here. A sweet for my sweety. Don't get too intellectual out here. They's all backward.'

'Looks sophisticated to me. A fine spot for us civilised folk,' Cindy harrumphed at me.

'You ain't civilised, and y'all never will be, hussy,' I teased.

She stuck out her tongue at me and put the candy in her mouth. 'Mmmm, this is mighty tasty.'

'Just keep sucking. I'll go find a place for us.'

Many people from all over crawled around the street. Horses with carts, more heavy-laden than ours, trundled along, with occupants hanging out the back. Finely dressed folk and bums intermingled together as one unit.

I did some exploring, when my eye caught a signpost that read *The Farr-Out Saloon.* The name intrigued me, so I went in...

... along with the wife, horse and cart...

... then thought better. 'Wait here,' I ordered.

'Yes, sir.'

I shook my head at the oddities of the love of my life. The inside of this place milled and bustled with custom. Billiards and card tables provided lively gaming, and drinks flowed like the waterfalls we'd passed on the way.

The lady of the house stood tall, with bright red hair (*or was it a wig?*), and a multicoloured dress with a frilly red border (probably to match with her hair). Upon clearer inspection, I realised that there was a man inside and the dress was a front. Wow... *it sure explains the name of the place...*

Bravely, I went up to the counter. 'Hello. Do you have any rooms for the night?'

'I'm on duty, what's the password,' came the funny reply.

'Ummm, I did not know there was one. If you're not vacant, then tell me so,' I spoke impatiently, just begging for a quick lie-down.

'Ah, you're a new bug. We do have rooms. How many are you?'

'It's the wife, myself and a horse.'

The proprietor replied, 'The horse would have a room to himself out in the rear stables.'

I sniggered... the gaiety of the moment had taken its toll upon me.

'What's so funny,' came another off-answer from the owner.

'Sorry. It was the way you said it.'

'You're not from around here, are ya sonny?'

'Good God, no. I'm from Chicago... good old Chicago. My family's been travelling West for years.'

'Sounds like you carried the ball yourself and survived the ordeal.'

'I've had my innings, yeah,' I smiled.

'Yeah,' she reflected, 'The Midwest... what an oasis. I'm from there myself. Farawcett, Muddens District.'

'Where's that?'

'In the far-off dunes of Ohio, or so they say. Small town, practically unmarked.'

'I see. I'm Amber Daye.'

The attendant smiled back. 'I'm Maxine Farr. Now, I need you to sign my register. I like to keep up with who stays at my establishment.'

'How d'you do,' I muttered, filling in the paperwork. I then looked up. 'Do you always dress like this?'

'Oh sure,' Ms Farr scoffed. 'Keeps the heat out.'

'And the other side in, eh?'

She hollered with laughter. I gave Ms Farr the book and she read aloud, 'Mr and Mrs Amber Daye. Nice couple.'

'Thanks. How much for the room and board, if you do such.'

'We never bore our customers, as there is too much to do. Between gambling, shooting and fist-fighting, there's not a moment to spare.'

'I did not come here to indulge in such trivialities. I am very tired, my horse and wife need a rest.'

'That will come to two dollars... one for the room, one for the horse.'

'That includes horse feed?'

'Horse feed is plentiful in these parts, so we don't charge much. It's included in the price.'

I paid the monies. 'I'm much obliged to you.'

'Okay,' she fumbled looking through the key press. 'That's room 321.'

'Oh, what about the meals?'

'For an extra dollar, you can have dinner and breakfast, all in the comfort of *The Farr-Out Saloon*,' Ms Farr stated proudly.

I dug in again and brought out another dollar. 'That's for me and the wife.'

'I know. You already paid for the horse. Bring him out back and we'll look after him.'

I put the key in my pocket and went outside to unhitch the horse. There were stables out back, as she said, and I left him with a circular-spectacled attendant called Ranger, wearing a military cap.

I then met the wife. 'We're going in. I've got the key.'

Cindy and I returned and went upstairs. Ms Farr waved to us. I waved back.

'That's either the ugliest woman I'd ever seen or that's a man playing dress-up,' Cindy whispered discreetly.

I scolded back, 'It's a man, now hush up!'

I opened the door and we entered the room with ourselves and sparse items we had on us. It was no different than *The Three Bells*, but it will do.

At this point, I didn't care. I flopped down onto the bed... ah, what a while it has been since...

... soon I dropped off, snoring quite loudly...

... to the indignation of Cindy.

'Amb-- oh, never mind.'

She surrounded me with her loveliness and, just like me, soon fell asleep. We slept pretty soundly for the next few hours.

CHAPTER VIII

That night, we had the meal Ms Farr had boasted about. It was quite good and always a pleasure to eat civilised rather than in the wilderness. Tender beef steak with a side of vegetables and potato, with a nice whipped cream style dessert.

Once we'd finished, we took a walk outside to look at the stars. Conversation did not breed upon our lips. We just stared jointly upward and the feelings between us were getting heavier and heavier.

The night sky was bold and brash as my little Cindy, with whom I was eager to bed...

... later on...

... which we did.

The American dream came full circle,
Never to run out of steam,
And like molten California lava,
I surged through a massive quarry,
Full of...
Amen.
My love, she got sloshed
On the backwoods of me
In the time it took
To outdala the century.
I wanted to see her
Race through me.
I lit her candle
And felt myself surge within her.
I got so excited
The hairs-by-the-cob had stood on end.

The body shown forth
The roughness of the earth,
And we fell into a pool of unlimited glory.

'Give me an inflection to remember you by and I'll remember everything,' she exclaimed.

'Hell kid, I maybe the gunpowder of your life, little Cindy,' I answered, 'But I didn't mean to blast your pardon.'

The vaults of hope were overcrowded when she said, 'Ye just blasted y'way right through me and gave me an eyeful of wow!'

I curled in violent repose. 'I know where they flavour cometh.'

She stopped her enslaved panting. 'I want to experience my pleasure in your presence and flavour your world...'

... so we did that, too...

... and enjoyed every minute.

We finished our bit, well into the night. The wind was talking to itself again, and picked fights with angry shutters and doors.

Yet, we didn't mind.

We let it go.

I put my arm around the dear one and gave her a warm cuddle and kiss. She turned to kiss me and quietly regained her sleep.

The next morning after breakfast, we said goodbye to Ms Farr and carried out onto further pastures galore.

The horse was fed.

We were fed.

Cart intact.

Life intact.

We were most happy and ready to push on...

... when suddenly, an Indian had wished to join us. He looked a bit wanting, his long hair was scruffy with several day's worth of dirt, and his face was handsome, but tarnished from travelling. He wasn't very young, but not too old, either. I noticed some townsmen staring at the fellow and it looked like they'd been in a scuffle together with him. Relations between Indians and whites were strained at the best of times, but there were exceptions...

... *however, this wasn't one of them.*

I had a thought, but thought I'd better ask first.

I said to him, 'Bit out of the way, ain't it?'

'Nawh, just had small picking from the townsfolk here, but I'm alright. I was hoping you could help me, just as much as I think you could use some company, maybe assistance,' he replied.

That seemed weird, but I allowed him to join us.

He took his place in the cart beside Cindy.

I asked, 'What's your name, son?'

'Whatho.'

'Interesting name,' Cindy gaped.

'Yes, it must date centuries,' I smiled.

'Well, it... umm...no... it's not like that,' Whatho argued.

I insisted. 'So what's it mean, then?'

Whatho looked embarrassed. My father, Novolace overheard some English-speaking settlers saying *'What ho!'* and thought it'd make a good name.'

I sighed. *At least, there was humour in our carriage.*

Whatho looked at Cindy. 'He your boss?'

'He's my husband. We got married by a priest from St Jacquet.'

'Oh, the Mission. I've heard of it. That's Whithog's territory, isn't it?.'

Cindy answered, 'Yes. Chief Whithog looked after me for many years. I was a runaway. I ran away from my grandparents back East. I had the option to marry Amber or be sent back. I'd be damned if I'd be sent back.'

'So you are...,' Whatho paused.

'Cindy Daye and Amber's drivin' at front.'

'Proud couple.'

'I think so,' Cindy engaged the Indian. 'Are you married?'

'Not yet. Taking it easy. It's not that I haven't tried, you see.'

Another sigh left my lips. 'You'll find someone. I did.'

'Do you work?' Cindy interjected.

'I spent much of my life outdoors, hunting and overall roughing it. I hear the animals at night, baying at the wind and the moon, watching for opportunity to move into life's secret cares.'

'With those credentials, you'll do fine with us,' Cindy mused.

'Secret cares,' I sniggered, 'You are as poetic as my Cindy here.'

Whatho couldn't make out what I meant. 'My people are very well spoken, with a bit of benelephants herding nearby.'

'Don't worry Whatho, I've got a flavoured way of talking, too,' she confessed, then cried aloud, 'Benelephants?!!'

'Yes, they are a most dastardly herd. They sneak up on you and before you get to shoot, they trample all over your meanings.'

I stopped the cart to compose myself. 'Would you excuse me?'

Whatho waved me on. 'By all means.'

I ran to the nearest tree to relieve myself. I was near to bursting after so much laughter erupted from the odd conversation we were having.

I went back and asked Cindy if she needed to go.

'Amber Daye,' she protested, 'I ain't no dog and I can't just piss any ol' where. I'm a lady. *You* made me a lady!'

Whatho showed some concern. 'Is there something I'm missing here?'

'Nah,' I assured him, 'Just asking my dearest if she needed to, you know...' I pointed at the tree where I'd been.

'Women,' the Indian shook his head and chuckled.

Cindy got annoyed. 'What are you laughing about?'

'You are very picky, ain't ya,' I observed, my heart racing from merriment.

She then got down from the cart and stomped her way toward the tree, but went further to a hedge of a larger kind to do her bit for the environment...

... and soon emerged thereafter.

'Better,' I cooed.

She carried on pouting. 'Yes. Nyahh!'

I grabbed her and planted a cool kiss on her lips…

… but she didn't respond well and I cried out, 'This is like kissing a stone; what's your problem?'

'I'd rather blow the stone,' she hissed in return. 'The dang thing's too far for me to kiss!'

'Short spot,' I called, as I saw her heading back to the cart to take her seat.

She stuck her tongue out me, and we fooled about for the moment before setting off travelling again.

Whatho was most fascinated at our behaviour towards one another.

'My father would have loved to meet you and your dear wife. He was most intrigued by the customs of white men.'

'We have nothing to hide, yet there's nothing to watch,' I stated.

'I think there is. The two of you going off on each other, play-fighting. I'm surprised you don't get physical.'

'Why use force, when the mind's all you need,' I answered, then turning to Cindy, 'Right, honey?'

'Assuming you got one,' she responded flippantly.

'Ah, the trappings of matrimony travelling Westward,' I crooned...

... and realised what a swinging time I had with Cindy.

CHAPTER IX

Several more weeks had passed... we entered another area, unknown to us, as we'd never been out here before. We were getting closer; Whatho, Cindy and I were continuing our Westward journey, despite the unfamiliarity of the place. The travails that befell us were enormous, but with our Indian friend's ingenuity and my perseverance, I reckoned we'd make it.

One day, a group of horsemen were spotted by Whatho, who thought they were following us. I could not figure out, for the life of me, as to why we were being trailed. I was aware that Cindy left her family a long time ago and Chief Whithog would have taken care of any subsequent snoopers. Surely no one back East had jurisdiction *here*, in these unknown Territories. I remember what Whithog said about how he had dealt with that previous Sheriff. It was quite a colourful yarn, but I trusted he meant what he said. True, the Sheriff never came after her again, and we were fine thus far.

And there was no reason for anyone else to look for her anyway...

...yet, the warning of the snake came true.

My curiosity was ruffled and I leapt out of the cart to meet the horsemen. I was feeling queasy and I looked out at Cindy, whose face shone the colour of continued torment. Whatho mistakenly thought it was *him* they were after. He remained silent, in case it were so.

One of them dismounted and we met on the same level. 'Are you Amber Daye?'

I swallowed hard. 'Yes.'

'Do you realise you are harbouring a runaway by the name of...,' he paused to read the notice, 'Cynthia of the Growling Sky?'

I cried in distress, 'How dare you!'

'Well, that's the last recorded name we have for her from the last place she resided back East. The original name cannot be pronounced properly; this is the closest thing we've got.'

'This woman here is my wife, Mrs Cindy Daye.'

'We were sent by her family, who are still looking for her.'

'You mean those grandparents of hers? They have NO rights to her. This lady is MINE,' I insisted.

Another horsemen piped up, seeing past the ruse. 'So this is the girl in question?'

I spat mutilated fire at him. 'She's not yours to take. Legally, she is mine.'

'Prove it.'

I fumbled through my pockets and waistcoat. I came across a bit of paper and read it. *Yep, this is it.*

I showed the fella the certificate.

'This was done on an Indian encampment. This is not real.'

'It's real to me,' I explained. 'We went through a proper Christian ceremony by one of the priests from St Jacquet.'

'I don't care what ceremony you went through.'

'We're heading out, whether you like it or not,' I argued.

'You ain't going anywhere, and we're taking the girl back to her Eastern family.'

No, I would not let that happen. I reached for my gun, when a shot was fired...

... straight into me.

I slumped forward, turned and leaned against the cart, slowly dying.

Cindy screamed in horror, 'Amber!'

Whatho held her and found an extra gun in the cart to give to her.

'You know what to do ol' girl,' he said.

She got off the cart, concealing the gun in her waistband. Another man took her and found the weapon. Cindy started crying and was scared beyond hope.

Whatho got off the cart and tried to play heroics...

... when another shot rang out.

The horseman who held Cindy had collapsed from the odd bullet, as Whatho threw his knife into the initial horseman who was questioning me...

... two down, one to go...

... and the last horseman, seeing two of his comrades killed before him deemed it futile to continue to press the situation...

... and, furthermore, fled the scene...

... but he did not go far, as Cindy took back the gun from her assailant and shot that bastard down forever.

She ordered Whatho to send for a doctor, then knelt by my side.

'Amber, Amber,' she sobbed, holding me.

I barely spoke; the blood filled my mouth faster than words. 'Cindy...'

I soon fell silent...

A loud cry had emitted from my dearest, as the only one she had ever loved, died in her arms. She howled for blood and sin upon any folk that would mess with her now. She grieved bitterly and felt she'd return East after all, just to put a cold, sweet bullet into the heads of those blasted grandparents!

But through her tears came the hope of a much better idea.

A man had emerged through the smoke and the sunny haze.

'Beggin' yer pardon, ma'am, you look dishevelled. May I help?'

'Gosh,' Cindy gasped, 'Whatcha doing 'ere way out in these here territories?'

'Oh, just wanderin'... like you folks,' he calmly replied.

Cindy snapped at the gentleman. 'We ain't wandering, we's heading West!'

'Youse travelling, I can see. Shame about that run-in. You shot 'im pretty good. I watched ya.'

She blushed. 'It was a lucky shot. Usually I'm bad with a gun. Did you shoot the fella that held me up?'

The Stranger quietly smiled and said nothing in return. He had seen the corpse laying beside Cindy and examined it.

'He your husband?'

'Duh,' spewed Cindy, still crying.

'Okay, okay, I get it.'

He continued the examination.

Cindy waited in anticipation, refusing to believe her husband was killed. 'Can you revive him?'

The Stranger looked up at her. 'Now, if I were a regular doctor, you'd best be preparing for a funeral. Out here in the wilderness, they's pretty bad, since the animals and scenery show no mercy on Christian souls, nor bodies...'

He paused, reflecting, '... but I ain't your average doctor. I'm a specialist. I've got some handy tools I bring along with me, in case I'm in need of them to help others, including that restless soul you call your husband.'

Reality stepped into her conscience. 'But he's been dead a few minutes. How can you bring him back? You can't!'

She was so sceptical!

The earthen eyes of the Stranger flashed open. 'Oh, can't I, eh? You'll see. Just do what I ask and we'll have you on your way in no time.'

'So you're operating here? Now?'

'The sooner the better, if you want to get him back so badly... and I know you do!'

He smiled and prepared himself for the task.

Cindy then enquired about Whatho.

'He'll find his own way. Fetching a doctor 'fore it's too late, as you ordered, but it takes time out here, don't it?'

'So he thinks, cos you're a doctor.'

'Correction, my lady, I'm a specialist,' the Stranger grinned. 'Oh, I say Whatho will find a new destiny, if he hadn't met one already, or perhaps he'll return to you. Now, hand me my bag over there.'

She picked up the black handled bag of hope, gave it to him, and found the discarded marriage certificate laying aside, and put it inside her blouse...

... next to her heart.

The Stranger fiddled around to fetch the wanted instrument.

'You see this here implement?'

Cindy peered at the elongated object. 'Yes.'

'Well, this at the top is a magnet. I'm going to extract the bullet out using this newfangled piece of equipment. A magnet attracts all kinds of metallic pieces and this one here's got surgical strength.'

'You'd be first in line for recruitment in the next war,' Cindy commented.

'Yes, indeedy... with the way these States are acting up, it'll be no wonder if I get called up for the sake of my crazy little device,' he mocked.

She giggled, then got serious. 'You could save many a man from destruction.'

'That's what I'm aiming at, though it is Man's wish to be destroyed. Now, hush up and let's get your husband back.'

Cindy let the Stranger do his work. She assisted him when asked, and left him be when told to.

The wounded area was uncovered and it looked wanting.

'Hand me my bottle,' he ordered.

She took it out. 'It's whisky!'

'Yep.' The Stranger took a quick swig, then spat it out upon the wound. He took a cloth, wiping up the blood, to go in and find the bullet.

'There she is,' he said. 'Now watch this.'

He took the magnetic piece and placed it into the cavity.

A small metal-on-metal sound was heard. Slowly, the item was lifted away from the body, taking the offensive bullet out of the system.

'There y'go. A nice, rounded-off bullet to keep for heck knows.'

Cindy took the bullet, which led to my silence and stared in awe.

'Doesn't look so bad when it's in this state, does it?'

'Doesn't look as bad in any State of a Winchester '77,' the Stranger joked, in a rather peculiar manner... 1877 was some years away.

He did a further clean-up job and put a bandage on the wounded area. Cindy watched as the Stranger laid both his hands on the bandage and said a prayer...

... when suddenly...

... I regained consciousness, as if to awaken from a very deep sleep.

I heard myself say, 'Where am I?'

Cindy rushed to hug me. 'Amber Daye, you're back!'

'Whoa, careful,' the Stranger warned, 'It's still tender there! Go easy on yer fella.'

'Oh, sorry.' She lightened the hug...

... but I knew she meant it.

She then asked the Stranger, 'What do I owe you, sir? This here's must have been a real live-one for ya.'

'Nothing,' the Stranger replied. 'You two just go on Westward, as you've been doing. I heartily recommend you ditch the horse and cart, though, and take a train. There's a station not too far from here. I can takes ya there.'

'Many thanks.' I got up to shake the Stranger's hand. An odd feeling had come over me afterwards. 'You know, you remind me of someone I knew... know... when I attend chur--...'

I stopped dead in my tracks, *literally.*

'You're not...,' I gaped at the Stranger...

... who then duly instructed me to keep it in my holster and hush it.

'I... I don't know what to say,' I continued rambling.

Cindy got pragmatic... *typical!*

'Please excuse my husband. After all, it's not like everyday you awake from being dead and stuff. He's just havin' a revelation. Would make sense in this sunshine.'

'But... I did... I was... dead... and... you're...'

I nearly fainted.

The Stranger caught me in agreement, as well as saving me from falling upon the ground. 'You certainly were, and I most certainly AM. My magnetic strip and whisky saved your life. Faith and Heaven did the rest.'

I dropped to my knees and exclaimed, 'My Lo-...'

'Awh, shut-up, don't make a to-do list over it,' the Stranger insisted. 'Look, I've got two tickets and fifty bucks for you, in exchange for the horse and cart. Getchaselves West as planned. I'd recommend Bravada City, near the Pass of the Sacred Memento. They need settlers out there to work the mines and such. Fort-building is also in the works. Y'all go on out there. It's your destiny, Amber and Cindy Daye.

Cindy got worried. 'What about my grandparents?'

'They'll be dealt with and youse never have to pay mind to them again.'

'You sure talk funny, if you say you are who you are, sir,' she added.

The Stranger took no offence. 'Just the way to blend in, I suppose. If I shot my mouth off like it was a couple a Millennia ago, who knows? Best keep it slow, simple, and shut-it. Let's get to the cart and take you to the station.'

I was still at a loss for words and took the back seat with Cindy instead. I let the Stranger do the driving.

My pallor did not go unnoticed by her...

... and she remarked, 'Amber Daye, you look like you'd seen a ghost!'

'I dunno, sweety, it's... it's...,' I stammered and my head fell on her lap.

'Men,' she giggled.

The Stranger giggled too, especially at the way I had reacted to him.

When we reached the station, known as the Shonnen-Glenfall Exchange, we said our goodbyes.

I wondered, 'Will we see you again?'

'In your heart, and in your life, I'll be with you. Be a good boy, Amber Daye, and look out for your family,' the Stranger advised.

He pointed at Cindy's tummy and it was revealed that she was pregnant.

My eyes flew open. 'Cindy, why didn't you tell me?'

'Cos you'd died on me, remember, duh! Anyway, I thought it best to get a second opinion.' She stared at the Stranger.

'You're a good people... the type of people we need out West to get the new nation going. You help out now.'

'Right,' I smiled, knowing the joys I had to come.

'Many thanks, and we'll remember you in prayers,' Cindy said, shaking his hand.

'I'll remember y'all on the Day. Sees ya 'round, folks.'

The train soon arrived and we boarded it, leaving behind the Stranger, the bullet, the horse, the cart and all the shit we'd gone though in the past together.

CHAPTER X

We boarded the train at the Shonnen-Glenfall Exchange and left the misery of slower travel behind us. I thought about that kindly Stranger, who saved me from that mortal bullet wound and eased all our minds to *get-on-with-it*-Westward. I wondered if I'd see him again, but knowing who he really Was, I thought better of it, and figured time at a church service would satisfy this.

Now that I was settling down with Cindy, I figured I would become part of a wider community of folk...

... I'd be a founder, too...

... a settler, rancher, or perhaps a farmer...

... but, I would be what I always had been...

... *a man.*

I looked around the train compartment, scanning over the tired faces of the massive bulk of humanity. Many were restless, bored, sleeping, and mostly relieved at the fact that there was a *quicker* way to travel, in general.

Suddenly, a black fellow approached us and sat opposite from me. He looked very flashy and very rich indeed... though I dared not to enquire of this. His three piece suit of the period made my plain and tacky garb pale in comparison.

He extended his hand. 'What'd y'say, pardner?'

I was taken aback by the forward confidence of such a person and exchanged greetings. 'Howdy.'

'I'm Sherman Tankard-Jefferson. I've come from the East, looking for opportunity.'

'Aren't we all?' I smiled, introducing ourselves. 'I'm Timothy Ambrossi Daye and this is my wife, Cindy.'

'Hi,' he waved. 'Ambrossi... you Italian?'

'Partly. It was an ancestor's name. I am predominantly Irish. You may call me Amber.'

'Please to meet you. Y'know, I've got big plans out West. I'm a businessman. Everyone's hogging up the Big Time back East, so, I thought, I could be the first out here to clean them out!'

This guy had to be kidding!

I exhaled, 'Ah. You sound like you are most certain. Wouldn't you come up against competition? What do you specialise in?'

He belted, as if on cue. 'Mattresses!'

His monosyllable outburst stirred my little Cindy. She sniffed, and opened her sleepy eyes.

She then looked at me, 'Who's that, Amber? He sure look fancy.'

'This here is Mr Tankard-Jefferson. He's going to make it Big. He thinks he could grant sweet dreams in the West.'

'Ain't nothing like a sweet dream with you, Amber,' Cindy sighed.

'Oh yeah, you bet I could,' the man boasted, dismissing her comment. 'I also do interior design. I could make a shack look like a mansion. I also heard there's mining springing up, along with the railroads. A guy could make a fortune out here!'

'Or lose it,' I muttered.

He ignored my comment... *typical!* 'Call me Sherman. I see your wife is expecting. Bit young, ain't she?'

'Not as young as you think,' I gave her a smile and rubbed her tummy.

A bit of silence passed us and I looked out the window. The prairies turned into a widespread desert and I knew we were getting closer. I saw some Indian encampments, with a few making a pass at one of the passing trains, trying to interfere with its progression. Yet progress was determined to plough past the continental divide, and soon enough, we crossed into the boundary into California.

It would take more time to get to the place suggested by the Stranger and a few weary stops hindered us for a good while.

Sherman asked, 'Where y'all gettin' off at?'

'We're headed for the Pass of the Sacred Memento, to a settlement called Bravada City. Someone told me there'd be work in the mines,' I replied.

'I'm heading for 'Frisco. There's probably a demand for mattresses and home furnishings in such a place. I can see the Big Time headin' out there.'

I smiled and thought about his bravado... *maybe he could join us instead?*

'Would you like to come with us?'

'Nawh, that ain't for me. Small poky townships don't turn me on. I came from a small poky township in the South, then headed North. I wanted to better myself and took the Tub Man Line. I got what it takes to make it.'

'I think you will, especially with these budding communities that need a place to sleep. I wish you the best of luck.' I shook his hand. 'Maybe we will meet again sometime.'

'Maybe,' Sherman muttered, with the intensity of success in his voice. 'But I doubt it.'

'One never knows.'

Shortly, the train stopped at Eldorado Pass, which was not far from the Pass that we were heading for. From there, we had to make our own way to Bravada City.

We left Sherman Tankard-Jefferson to roll-over himself in his dreams. I honestly meant the best for him, but I reckoned it'll be a long-haul journey.

With the little money we had, along with the money we got from the Stranger, for the horse and cart, we spent some of it on a horse to take us to our final place...

... and this time, we wouldn't have to go too far.

After a quick refreshment for our souls and bodies, with a bite to eat along the way, we rode on into the California wilderness to find our way to success...

... not necessarily by the Bay, mind.

It was not too far a ride and we rested for a bit when a familiar face came to the fore.

'Hiya Amber. Didn't think you'd see me again, now, did ya?'

It was Whatho.

I stuttered in response from shock. 'B...but, we left you back in the unknown Territory.'

'Ah well,' he shrugged, 'An Indian with connections here and there. You know how it is... I saw you on the passing train.'

Cindy was just as surprised. 'I told you to get a doctor and you'd just left us.'

'Ummm... I didn't intend to leave you folks. I did find one in the end but he was new to the scene and was unfamiliar with mortal wounds. I then got roughed up by some local gangs who didn't like Indians; they ran me out of town, but not without putting me in their cells overnight... then I made my way alone, ran into fellow tribesmen who also spotted you on the trains passing by. I joined them, and here I am.'

Whatta story!

'Wow,' Cindy mouthed.

'I see you recovered from your ordeal, Amber,' Whatho noted.

I smiled. 'Awh, it's alright. You wouldn't believe any of it, anyhow. Someone kind had looked after me.'

I looked up at the sky and pointed toward the heavens.

Whatho's eyes lit up in recognition. 'Oh, that. We sometimes get visitations from the Spirit world too, but it's usually from the bottle. Someone tells us about it the next day after they've woken up. Very hard to believe, most of it.'

I squirmed and attempted to explain what happened and the Stranger Who saved my life...

... when Cindy cut me off. 'Wait Amber, let me tell him.'

'The floor's yours, dear,' I agreed and let the sweet girl ramble onwards.

She began, 'This guy said he was a specialist, unknown as to what; he didn't say. He showed me a device that used magnetic energy to pull the bullet out, which he did.'

'So that's what you call 'em... *magnets*,' Whatho chuckled. 'My people saw a similar item that draws metal to it. We called it the Great Grabber.'

'After the bullet was out, the Stranger had cleaned the wound with whisky. He drank some of it and spilled the rest on Amber,' Cindy giggled.

I freaked out. 'Whisky? He used whisky on me?'

'Yes Amber,' Cindy recalled, 'He used it on the wound, then said a prayer when you came 'round.'

'I've heard of that too. Must be the Spirit inside the liquid; it's said to have healing qualities.'

'Guess human habits ain't a bad thing, when done right,' I said.

'So it wasn't just progress, but old fashioned spirits that took you around,' Cindy concluded.

'Well, whatever it was that fellow did for us, it was mighty good of him. He gave us some money for that horse and cart we lugged about earlier, and train tickets.'

'So you've been through a lot,' Whatho muttered.

'Not to mention we met this guy on the train who was a real scream. He was a black fellow who made his business in mattresses,' she blurted.

Whatho quipped, 'So he can put us all to sleep, is that it?'

We had a laugh about it when Whatho apologised to us for not being there.

'You can make it up to us and work,' I offered. 'Cindy will need much help.'

The Indian looked at my wife and noticed a small roundness about her.

'Very good, man, very good.' Whatho shook my hand and gave me a hug. 'Sounds well to me.

We left to find Bravada City, where our new lives awaited. We took turns walking and riding the horse.

I wanted to give preference to Cindy, out of respect, but she wouldn't have it and felt walking would help strengthen her where it counted.

It was a few days before we finally made it to the City. The main strip was teeming with people and bustling with activity of many kinds. The streets were stretched out all the way toward a mountain known as the Mountain of Pale Lava, set firmly in the distance. It was a dead volcano, the spew of which happened millennia ago; the resulting white surface had given the mountain its name.

So, there was no threat from the fiery demons that lived inside...

... or so the Natives thought.

The area was very land-rich, indeed, and many people regarded it a blessing and volunteered to take up a ploughshare of the land... hungry for a land mass to call their own, or pass onto heirs or Trustees of Wills. Land Registry offices were crammed with many hopefuls who wanted a stake into their own futures.

I didn't rush into it, though I strayed around like a prairie dog, just looking and watching...

... ready to pounce on opportunity.

Whatho spotted a saloon and we were in need of refreshment. We hitched the horse to a post, where a water trough lay for him to drink, and went inside to order drinks for the rest of us...

... and this time, Whatho was left in peace.

'Some fellow tribesmen made a stand to defend themselves, now run this town,' Whatho explained. 'Others who didn't make it, got sent to the confines of reservations.'

I asked, 'Does the mountain in the far distance mean anything to your people?'

'It is where the spirits lie in wait, and we commune with them when the white stuff glows more fiercely during summertime,' he replied.

'I think it would be good if your people could live there.'

'A few still do; there are tribesmen who feel likewise.'

Cindy sipped her drink and wondered where we were going to stay the night. I told her not to worry and gave her a kiss.

I got up to see the barman about such matters...

'Got any rooms for the night?'

The barman looked up from the register, where he was counting his money. 'Dollar per night. If you plan to settle, the Land Registry office is just across the road.'

'Thank you,' I replied, turning away to return to my family.

'Hey wait,' the barman called. I went back to the bar. He continued, 'There's a mighty fine property in the back of the forest that has a working windmill. No one's taken it up yet and it's sittin' around doing nothin'. It could harvest a great deal and could make you a lot of money. I'm friends with the land owner and willing to give you an opportunity to buy it.'

'You don't say,' I responded, thinking heavily, and sceptically. 'I'll think about it and get back to you.'

'No need to rush, but you may wish to consider quickly. Talk to Mr Haggard at the office and tell 'im Mr Carroll sent ya.'

I waved with gratitude back at him and sat down with Cindy and Whatho to discuss the matter. We still had some money left over; this windmill could make a beautiful home for us to settle and our child would live in a ready-made place.

No foolin' about looking and moving all the time.

When we finished, I had Whatho watch over the horse, and Cindy and I went to the Office of Land Registry to enquire about that windmill property (to find whether or not it was full of hot air), and I mentioned the barman.

The clerk, Mr Haggard, recalled, 'Oh, Mr Carroll is full of it, but he *is* friends with the owner.'

'He boasted highly about the property,' I remarked.

'Well, how much you got? No one's been able to take on the place, because it is too quirky for average folk. You don't look average to me,' Mr Haggard observed.

'We're not,' I smiled back.

'Thought not. No offers for the place had come up either, so, what you got? There's no competition, so...'

No competition... I wondered... *but we needed to live somewhere.* I looked hard and long at the clerk's desk, dishevelled like a woman's hairstyle first thing in the morning. The ink blotter had written figures, doodles, notations, covering its surface, like organised graffiti cementing people's futures.

I sighed heavily. I went into my pockets and counted how much we had left.

'I've only got forty dollars.'

'I'll take it. The owner left it semi-furnished and there is some livestock for you to work with,' Mr Haggard mentioned to me. 'If you want to put your special stamp on the place, that's your business.'

'Sounds like he was desperate to leave such a nice place,' I thought aloud, giving Mr Haggard the payment.

'A job was waiting for him back East and he had family there too, so... at least you'll have a place for you and your lady. You wouldn't want to sleep in the streets. She doesn't look fit to rough-house a barn.'

'She's pregnant,' I explained.

'Just as well. Sign here.'

I was given the Deed and signed accordingly. I folded it up and put it in my pocket.

'Good luck to you and yours, Mr Daye.'

I waved goodbye to Mr Haggard and went out to look for the horse. I saw that Whatho remained with the horse, still hitched and watered from the trough beside him. I gave the beast a pat on the head and he neighed back at me. I removed the rope from the post and mounted him. Cindy and Whatho walked on each side, guiding him.

'Amber,' Cindy called out.

'Yes, my dear?'

'I think we could use a cart. This walking is getting to me.'

Poor girl... we were out of money, though, as we spent the last of it on that windmill property.

'Let's go home and we'll plan our next move,' I suggested. 'Would you like to hop on and ride in front of me?'

'Yeah!' Cindy climbed up on the horse, in front of me. It was a bit of a pinch with the saddle, but we managed just fine.

'Thanks, baby,' she said, kissing me.

Whatho smiled too, and firmly held the rein.

The rest of the journey was not too far as we thought...

... for before we knew it, we'd reach *Xanadune...*

... which was the name of that windmill.

CHAPTER XI

As a windmill, Xanadune looked the part, with wide white sails, with slots along each one, and the main body of the edifice was our living quarters. A few acres of land came with it, along with some livestock, given as part and parcel. It seemed like the West was an area of boom or bust. Sometimes you had to settle up and leave; other times, you could plant your roots here and live forever...

... which is what we were going to do!

At least, work was plentiful. I looked around and found a job at a gold mine. Whatho and Cindy looked after the domestic side, *as long as they didn't go domestic on each other!* Day after day, I slogged my pack out, working and hauling large amounts of gold out of the surface. It was difficult at times, but I confessed to enjoy it, as the money was good and as a bonus, we shared in some of it.

* * * * * *

Time passed and Cindy was nearly due. I wanted to help her out and be with her at the birth, so they let me go off work for a few days...

... and sure enough, when that time came, a little lady was born unto us. We called her Amber Leigh Daye. I was flattered that my nickname was to be her proper name. She was average sized, not too big, nor small... she was just right, just like my Cindy.

The farm was taking shape around Xanadune, too. The lucky few animals left behind had been maintained well by us and shortly, they went in season. Our little family of many beings grew and we all had our hands full...

... but mine were full of gold dust, which I was supposed to get back to soon.

Life at home was pleasant enough; we grew our own fruit and vegetables; Cindy took the apples and strawberries and made jam out of them. We went to the markets for fresh meats, and the cooking skills she learned amongst the Indians had served her well. Even Whatho brought to the table his self-taught skills, and the cultural fusion was at its best.

Little Amber Leigh grew up well and enjoyed helping Cindy. They were like two peas in a pod. I felt we were a well-growing family. With the addition of a son we called Timothy Ross Daye (Ross for short), I felt completed and naturally expunged. It didn't mean, however, that we wouldn't try for more, later on. For now, we were a definite cohesive unit.

The months turned into years; the recent ones had brought with them much hardship for our nation. The already established Southern states had disagreed with their Northern neighbours and pulled out of the Union. The Northerners were unhappy with the Southern wish to expand slavery into the newer Territories. California was just as divided, with its own North and South interests and sympathies, respectively, reflecting those in the East. So everyone was at odds with one another and it looked like we'd have to fight over whose idealism was best.

Forts began to spring up to train troops (for the coming conflict), and quell Indian raids on recent settlements. Fort Bravada was built, not too far from Xanadune; it was a Unionist outpost and the commander of the fort, Nohmend Dexx, had come to me with regards to helping out the Cause, making use of my unique property. He had an idea of having us supply grain for food and we'd get payment from the government.

I thought Xanadune was just for show, but upon inspection during Dexx's visit, it appeared to be a working mill with a grindstone, found in the lower section of the property.

Soon enough, I had to put aside my pickaxe from the mines and got drafted into the Army. I was stationed at Fort Bravada, though I had the option to come join the fighting back East. I chose to remain at the Fort, near my family, and my knowledge of the area would prove useful, after living here for a good few years.

The Fort did not see much action, but for the many an Indian conflict that aroused the established settlements. Much of these uprisings had been quashed and the surviving Indians had been forcibly taken to government-run reservation sites. I personally did not like the fact they were just driven off and that we all could not live in peace with them. Our household had proven an Indian *can* live with white folk...

... but one Indian had called upon me, personally, to ask for my help.

An elderly chieftain from a local tribe of the 25th had sought me out at the Fort, led by the Spirits above, or the spirit within. His name was Hueronnamo. The commander disapproved of the idea, but allowed me to deal with the matter, as he saw I had a way with the Indians.

'Our lands are slowly being taken away from us. Many of my tribe were put on your reservations and those still with me are hoping we could remain where we are. We do no harm and want to live in peace, yet it is a piece of us that your people want,' Hueronnamo lamented.

I sighed and remembered the Mountain of Pale Lava. 'There's a mountain in the far distance of Bravada City, all covered in white.

'Someone had told me it is where the spirits lie in wait, there is communion with them when the white stuff glows at certain times of the year.'

'Our people and ancestors worshipped it for long time before other tribes made us spread outward and we'd lost touch with the Mountain.'
I winked, 'How would you like to get in touch with it again?'

'We would love to return,' he smiled, 'But your people are making it difficult for us to remain there. We want to be free!'

'And so you shall. I doubt the land is of interest to us, to my knowledge, so I do not see why you cannot live in the confines of the Mountain.'

'That would be most agreeable, but how will you convince your people?'

'I'll think of something. By hook or by crook, I'll get you there.'

Hueronnamo and I shook hands in agreement. *Commander Dexx had other ideas...*

'Those natives belong on the reservation, with the rest of their kind,' he scoffed.

I turned to him. 'I think you are just singling them out just for the sake of it. You are not interested in the land, you just want them cleared away, don't ya?'

'Now, don't be foolish, Lt. Daye, that's treason.'

I folded my arms. 'They were here first, you know.'

The commander walked away, fuming. 'It is not your decision. I let you talk, now let us do the rest.'

I still wasn't amused. 'It'll come to what it'll come to.'

I left the steady commander and thought of a plan to assist Hueronnamo's tribe.

* * * * * *

One night, I decided to leave Fort Bravada to find Chief Hueronnamo. I knew I was being defiant, and my actions could be misconstrued as treasonous, but...

... although I loved my country, I gave way to my fellow man...

... no matter who he was.

I managed to find the good Chief, who offered me some Indian clothes as a disguise.

'I think you would stand out in uniform, no?'

I laughed and threw the military apparel aside. 'Let's get your people together and go to the Mountain.'

Everyone was present and we walked in the night, through brush and tree-lined path. Nature was a good concealer, but a change of clothes added well to my presence. It was a true wilderness, and one worth fighting for, even if it was a fight given by the *other* side.

I wasn't going to just kill someone who just wanted to live in peace, or whatever; as long as they stayed civil...

... and in my opinion, I believed the Indians were as civil as they came...

... in their own way...

... *when unprovoked.*

However, the Commander of Bravada, Dexx, had caught unto my scheme and followed me with some foot soldiers...

... probably to arrest...

... or hang...

... *yours truly.*

Yet, I was undeterred, and one of Hueronnamo's warriors spotted the approaching soldiers and pelted him with an arrow. Other warriors saw their cue and did likewise, before the soldiers had time to shoot...

... and some did and got a few...

... Dexx included...

... but not me.

I had a hand with arrows, too, and got a soldier...

... which I wasn't very proud of...

... and it could probably lead to a court martial...

... or otherwise.

Hueronnamo got injured, but only a graze was revealed.

'I'll get up again,' he said, 'Now, let us continue our journey.'

Dismissing the earlier debacle, the Chief, myself and his tribesmen had followed the path along and soon, the white sheen of the Mountain loomed closer. Many had cheered their good fortune, others made comments and thanked me for my help.

'You saved us,' said one of them. 'We didn't think you'd care.'

Ah, but I did. 'We do... I do care. I cannot speak for my people, as they embrace alternative views, but I care enough to see you fulfil your lives and spirits.'

Hueronnamo couldn't thank me enough. He took off one of the many pendants of his regalia and hung it around my neck. The pendant showed a symbol of two people embracing, surrounded by protective arrows.

I blushed. *I did not deserve this.*

'For you, Amber Daye, an honourable adoptee of the 25th Tribe,' Hueronnamo announced.

I still blushed. 'Thank you. It's a lovely item. Many thanks and blessings go with you and yours.'

'Peace be upon you and your...,' the Chief hesitated. 'Do you have a tribe of your own?'

I smiled. 'Yes. I have my own... tribe. We call it a family. I have a wife and two children.'

'Ah, you have full house. May it remain full, and with many more. We pray for you from the Mountain of Pale Lava.'

I clasped my hands. 'And my prayers shall go to you, too.'

I recovered my military outfit, and returned to the Fort to find it still running, minus the group that went to search for me. The Commander was hit, and no one was really in charge at the moment...

... *it was too sudden.*

I quickly changed into my Army gear and sought out the next in command...

... if there was one.

Nobody said much to me, despite what I had done. The Army still needed my windmill for grain and decided to keep me on; it appears that they would not let go of something that would help out in the long run...

... at the very least, I did handle the Indians...

... but not in the way the government desired...

... it was good enough, as there were no subsequent trouble since.

My time with Hueronnamo was well justified and I wore his old pendant with pride...

... under my uniform, of course.

I continued my life working at the Fort, carrying out my orders and not acting contrary to the main interests thereof.

There wasn't much doing anyway, as no further problems came to date. Paper pushing was battle enough for me. Many of the clashes happened out East. After some time, I worked my way through; once peace had broke out, I got discharged and resumed my previous routines of work and family.

CHAPTER XII

A few years went by, into the 1870s and we, at Xanadune, were doing fine. The family was growing up well, but diggin' at the mines had taken its toll on me. Not that I minded, it was good solid work, sorely needed to keep us afloat. Yet, with the minimal payouts we got from the government for our grain and the chump change my dearest Cindy collected for her jams during market days, things did add up nicely...

... provided you saved it or spent it when needed.

Ross and Amber Leigh contributed greatly toward household chores, after going to school during the day. They took it in stride, knowing all hands were needed aboard our ship, as it were. Playtime was spent wholeheartedly when they met some school friends and hung out together, either in town or near the homestead. They sure grown up nicely, and made pleasant company, whiling away the evenings with us.

During one Christmas season, I decided to help out at church, preparing for their Yuletide activities. My spare time was spent working with the children and reading stories and poems to them. It gave me purpose in life to see the ones who will take-the-place, long after my time. Bravada City was certainly getting on in population, and seeing so many little ones warmed my heart. It was like seeing Ross and Amber Leigh all over again. I deeply enjoyed sharing myself to the children, who made a fine audience, indeed, but it was nothing like being with your own.

I watched them, the girls in frilly floral dresses, wrapped in pretty bows of decoration, and the boys showing off in their suited Sunday best. In a small, gas-lit dimmed room, with a Tree at the back, and the curtain slightly opened (just in case something magical happened), I sat in a rocking chair, like the elder gentleman that I was, be-suited and besotted with the excitement in the room.

My thoughts ran in the direction of my dearest wife, as I read, but I focused mainly on the juvenile crowd that sat (in a large group) before me.

We talked and had a laugh about what presents one would get and who would be the giver of them. I read various stories and poems of the season, the most popular being *'Twas the Night Before Christmas.* I told them Cindy and I had written a banner of a poem of our own, to which the children chimed...

'...yes, Mr Daye, please read it!'

And so I did…

Nothing matches like love in your trim
As colourful medical sutures on your skin.
I see you wrapp'd up in swaddling clothes,
Mixed up within a manger-full of pantyhose.
(Because your mother's on her own.)
I see you laying there in a makeshift cosy crib
Filled with straw
That the animals happily shared with you...
To which they said,
'There's plenty more!'
And then, as the stars twinkled in the Heavens,
Three bright sparks shining bright,
Thought to pay you a visit,
Tonight.
Giving you gifts of hope and glory;
(The power will come later.)
They sensed, incised, and tracked,
Seeing you into your future well...

Yet, there are those left behind,
And those that wish not to find.
Their lot has been cast aside,
As the love shone toward others
Outshined.

The children clapped wildly and praised the highly imaginative work.

'Get it published in the local paper,' one of the older children blurted out.

I blushed. 'Nawh, it is nothing. Just a silly rag between me and the wife.'

A girl shouted, 'But it is fantastic, Mr Daye. You should go to the editor of the paper and get it out for the season.'

'I'll think about it,' I smiled.

The time came to an end and we partook of the refreshments ranging from home-baked snacks and child-friendly drinks, it was a most worthy cause to cherish...

... and talk about later in life to their own children.

Once I returned home, the cause never glowed brighter.

'Amber,' Cindy cried, clutching my hand and embracing me.

'Cindy doll.' I returned the favour with a quick squeeze.

'Never thought you would be the church-nanny type. Reading the tykes to bed.'

'Could be my thing. This place makes you grow some. I read the poem.'

'Oh that,' she dismissed. 'Horse-shacks! I didn't think nothin' of it.'

'The children did,' I said, 'They suggested I publish the thing in the newspaper.'

'*The Bravada City Heartbeat?* You crazy; no way.'

'Maybe it could make us a bit more, you know,' I hugged and snuck a kiss on her neckline.

'You know what,' came the ubiquitous response.

I reflected on what was said...

... and took it as a joke.

'C'mon honey, it will be fun. To see our names in print,' I coaxed, drooling at the prospect.

'Oh awl right, I'm convinced. If young'uns will love it, then old folks like us would wallow in it,' she conceded.

Cindy, Cindy, Cindy...

Later on, I did get that poem out to the *Heartbeat*. The editor liked it, paid us $25 for it and had it printed in the following edition.

Our names glowed like wildfire and many in the town enjoyed the frivolity...

... easily dismissing it as good ol' seasonal hijinks...

... but they liked it anyway and thought it was an interesting take on the true meaning of it all.

Meantime, the government were still struggling with Indian raids and I got roped back to Fort Bravada to fix a solution, once and for all. My arrangement with them was mutual. I provided their food, they paid me... now they wanted me to go against those I admired and did not wish to find cause with...

... and I thought the matter was resolved years ago!

As the staff at the Fort knew I was clever with them Indian folk; I would not treat them with violent means...

... the Fort, though, didn't think so, and wished to commence fighting anyway, and perpetuate their upstart attitudes toward the Natives.

I stated there were to be no violent means; no conflict; no killing. We'd had enough of that during the late War, and I certainly did not want that again.

The new Commander, Lance Dexx (son of Nohmend Dexx), bellowed, 'If you think you could curtail them, I dare to think you could try; you won't live to see it through.'

What a challenge!

What an idiot, how he underestimated the little guy...

... me...

... not that I was little, you see.

They gave me the nod and I went about my business with the Indians. I thought far and wide about it and realised, if food works for the Army, what's to say it would not work for my Native friends...

... and then, I remembered Cindy's jam.

I informed him of my intention. He said I was crazy...

'... but good luck to youse,' he guffawed hysterically. 'Jam jars... he's going to appease Indians with jam jars!'

'Not any old jam jars... my wife's jam jars.' I folded my arms in defence of my most beautiful.

'Uhhh....,' the new Dexx turned tail when he realised my wife's jam was the *best* in Bravada City and that there was a high demand for it.

A short pause later, he said, 'You got it, just don't come back with an arrow up your butt.'

I walked out, and headed for home to collect the nectar that would distribute peace throughout the land...

... or in the immediate vicinity, at least.

With the handful of jars packed neatly in a bag, I saddled the horse and rode to the Mountain of Pale Lava in search of the 25th.

When I reached the 25th, among the other Indian tribesmen and their leaders, I announced my presence, and my offering to them...

'... and I present my wife, Cynthia Daye's Blessed, Fruited, and Spreadable Jam!'

The Natives responded, something like this:

'Does she take requests? I like raspberries.'

'Blueberries for me, please.'

'How about pemmican pate mixed with honey?'

I was quite overwhelmed at the responses. 'I've got strawberry,' I said, giving my gift to the nearest leader.

'Ohh, this will go nicely with the bread we just baked,' one tribesman exclaimed, already opening the jar, taking a taste. 'Holy Buffalo Fodder, this is tasty. Thank you, nice white man from afar.'

'It's Amber. Amber Daye, and thank you,' I smiled.

The Indians congregated around a table where their women brought out breadstuffs and, of course, out came the knives and the spreading began.

Chief Hueronnamo came out of his tent. 'Did someone say Amber Daye?'

I spun around, 'Aye, it's me.'

We embraced. 'Amber, I never thought I'd see you again. How've you been?'

'Good. I came by on behalf of my government again.'

His face became forlorn. 'You come to move us?'

'No no no,' I touched his arm. 'I've brought a peace offering.'

One of the Indian's shouted out, 'Chief, this jam is excellent. Come and try it.'

Hueronnamo was flabbergasted. 'Jam?'

'My wife's recipe. She's gotten good at making it and I convinced those at the Fort to offer it to you as a sign of goodwill.'

One of the ladies gave the Chief a slice with the holy spread. He bit in and chewed, contemplating the flavour source.

'Ummm, strawberry,' he nodded with approval.

'Yes,' I grinned eagerly.

'Your wife good cook. Makes good jam. Got cherry flavour?'

'I'll add it to the request list. Your people are very enthusiastic,' I replied.

He noticed the pendant he'd given to me from our last meeting.

'You wear that with pride, don't you?'

I looked down on the item and smiled. 'Yes, that I do.'

'No one ask about it in your group?'

'Why should they? Most of my folk know I handle relations with you. It is no surprise to them that I wear a token of esteem.'

'Although they may think you turn coat,' Hueronnamo added glumly.

'Nah, I'd never do that. I may like y'all, but I know my place is with...,' I paused.

'... your own kind and family. How are they, by the way?'

'Fine and growing well.'

We parted on excellent terms and I made it my business in future to supply them with Cindy's jams.

Later on, I informed Cindy about my peace offering.

'Foodstuffs always make good gifts, especially to those of a different culture. You can get to know them better through food. Everything revolves around the tummy. It always will. It is the nature of survival and I firmly believe the Indians are the survivalist type, after all they've been through.'

'After all *you've* been through,' I commented and gave her the request list.

She ignored the old memory. 'Guess my work's never done.' She got up to get a pan out and fetched the children to pick some more fruits.

Amber Leigh and Ross were laughing as they picked the fruits to further our united cause.

CHAPTER XIII

Another town nearby was gathering momentum. Mashton had a harsh start, with the current population dwindling to 4,069 when eight people were reported missing after the War. Since those meagre times, the new town boomed, when the mines in its locality struck gold. Strong personalities emerged in these plentiful times, and, in gratitude, they were holding a fair to celebrate their newfound status as a corporation and a growing concern.

So everyone in the community had geared toward the event. It took awhile in preparation, with many of us joining in, including Cindy's omnipresent jams.

It was a delightful fairground, with carousel rides, pony rides, various children's activities, and the odd re-enactment of the late War done by the actual soldiers who fought (and proud of their involvement). There were soldiers hanging about too, probably waiting for an audition. I overheard a couple of them talking...

... *and gained a snippet:*

'My wife, she's having the ol' Colonel Cold-Cuts for afternoon tea.'

'Didn't know she invited him.'

'Yeah, for old times' sake. She thought she'd be doin' the country a service.'

'What this country needs is a better train service. I heard the previous President wanted to ride one before he died.'

'Yessum, and he did... die, that is... and probably rode the train to Whereverville.'

The two men laughed; not a bright spark between them. *It was a wonder they'd survived the horrors of the War.*

'The government needs to do something about the railroads, though. We could use one to get to the Specific.'

'That's Pacific, you knucklehead, and they already did!'

A third party walked into the hilarity. 'Yeah, I heard they'd build one by the Killing Bite trail.'

'That's the mine, silly!'

'Yeah, but I think it will be time before they makes up their mind... they're as useful as a counsel of Christmas lights on a hot summer day!'

'There, you said it, Abner, not me!'

What a boring conversation, I sighed to myself and walked on.

In another section of the grounds, a troupe of army surgeons from the late War had presented a little something to pass the time by. One of them did some comic routines and another read a poem aloud, and it went something like this:

Painful suicides
And country brides,
Longing for their men;
The President
Is in his Den
Handing out favours
Between North and South.

From pink-laced politicians
To military admissions...
Of faith.
Amputating the rugged score,
Drugging out those who'd gone before
As a new patient arrives in tow.
Hitched to a beggar's cart,
Not feeling much, but nonchalance,
I think I'm now ready for bed.

The audience applauded, including us. There were other parts of the production as well, giving the usual re-enactments of experience, along with a jovial wing. The jokes were fun, but I liked that poem best...

... I saw that there was competition in the air, but I daren't send for the clarion...

... for my talent was private and seasonal.

I could not remember such a sparkling day like this. I thrived on the vibes that fed off other revellers and believed my folks would have been gosh-darn proud of me, just to have made it out here in the first place!

Amber Leigh and Ross took in their focus of activity and soon joined us for the afternoon.

'Had you seen that fella on the horse. Man, was he swervin', Ross exclaimed.

An excited tone hinted at my daughter as well. 'I liked the carousel the best.'

'You would. All girls like that stuff.'

'So what? I'm a girl,' Amber Leigh defended.

'That's sure obvious.'

'Nyahhh,' she stuck her tongue out at Ross.

Ross did likewise and added a raspberry for effect.

'Now, now, children. Hey, simmer down, please. No antics, y'hear,' I tried to separate them. 'The War has long been over, we don't need to start again.'

'He started it,' Amber Leigh pointed accusingly at Ross.

'I did not,' he protested.

My dearest intervened. 'It doesn't matter who started it. Just try to be civil, yeah?'

'Okay,' Amber Leigh backed down.

'Let's shake on it,' Ross offered.

They shook hands.

'Now play nice for Heaven's sake,' I ordered.

'Yes, sir,' both added and went off to watch the penny-a-piece card players.

I put my arm around Cindy. 'So much for our family gathering.'

'Oh, they're gathering all right,' she said, 'They're gathering momentum as we speak.

We whiled away the afternoon soaking up the California sunshine and those bustling vibes around us. It was good to spend time with the wife, as much as I could, considering my work took me away from her for many an hour.

My eye caught onto something or someone in the corner. Through the glorious haze of newfound municipality, I spotted something hot, buttered, glazed, lean, but couldn't tell if mean. The fellow walked about life as some kind of hen-hock. His suit was brown, with a silken tie and a blower in pocket sticking upward. The top hat couldn't climb any higher, and he was lucky the buildings were taller than he.

The irregular aspect about the fellow was that he looked like *me* and I'd never seen him before in my time, ever...

... except maybe in a mirror.

So what was the connection?

'Pa, Pa,' Amber Leigh approached me to give a hug.

I answered the call. 'Yes, my pet.'

In the corner of my eye, I could see this guy staring. Did he think I was hugging my other half, or did he hear correctly it was my girl? I felt protective and didn't want no fuss.

'Pa, I have something to tell you.'

I kept looking at the man. I wondered if *he* was the reason for my daughter's excitable outburst...

... I saw him eyeing her hungrily...

... but without the energy to pounce, or even kill.

Was it all innocent?

So, I asked, 'What, my dear?'

'I met someone. Would you like to meet him?'

'Meet who?'

'You'll see. It's that fellow over there. He was at the penny players and won a bit of prize money. We got talking and he asked if I was alone. I told him about you, Ma and Ross.'

'So it's meet the family time, eh? G'on, let's meet this friend of yours.'

I was unsure of the suddenness of her rashness, but I went along with the gag. I had hoped it would be just a quick flirty thing, stick to the business, and walk away *cleanly* sort of deal. My tummy fluttered, as I held her hand. Cindy followed and Ross was waiting at the building where this fellow-in-question also awaited our presence.

Amber Leigh gained her stride as she rode up to the person who would change the destiny of our family.

'Pa, Ma, Ross, I want y'all to meet Jonah Ebenezer Hathaway.'

Part II - Jonah Ebenezer Hathaway
(MID TO LATE-1800s)

CHAPTER XIV

It was a movement in time, I saw a young girl, nearly half my age, give or take a day or so. I've cut my prime with women within my many years of life, but she was exceptional. Not like a barkeep or a field worker, or a butch-type matron that looks at you funny the moment an interest sparked.

Most people saw me as one who aged gracefully and quietly in a doorway, with an ego to fill a square-rooted garden patch. I didn't care. Life was one thing after another. My family came from England back in the 1700s. They settled in New York and were loyal to the Crown during the Revolutionary era. They found most of those so-called Patriots hot-headed louts who didn't know what they were getting themselves into...

... but they knew what they wanted out of!

A family story was handed down proudly, when an antecedent of the cloth by the name of Jonas Hathaway had married an odd-ball colonial to a Redcoat. This colonial bitch had stifled plans for Independence and it cost us another 30 or so more years of British rule... with *them* bossing us around still. Although my family were of the Crown mindset, I became more of a Patriot at heart, even though I wasn't even born yet...

... but if I had, I'd know which side to choose.

I had heard weird stories about this colonist... a sad and angry case, with whom even the King sympathised. It was told she returned to England with her Redcoat husband and both served their Royal Master...

... well, good riddance to her, I'd say!

A generation later, my family moved West, as it was apparent that the newer group would be happier to live as citizens of the New Nation, once we freed ourselves from Britain in the 1812 conflict.

I was born Jonah Ebenezer Hathaway in 1840, during our exodus West, with no marker to provide for the occasion. I was a true-born Westerner. We were in it together, and I spat on the memory of the nation's earlier years, which could fill a spittoon with the usual sense of restless garbage.

I spent much of my time planning to make my way into this new world of experience. There was money to be made and I'd learned through years of hard graft that *anyone* could make it. I worked my way up, doing odd jobs here and there. I saved much of my earnings, for I lived with my folks until they died. I grew up pampered, but I grew up mean, too. I wanted a piece of the action and I became more focused on succeeding.

An interest in the railroads came my way and suddenly, one could invest in the new companies. I took some of my savings and did so. With the triumph of the railroads as the way of the future, I decided to continue the efforts. I went into new ventures and business, loving it when it paid off. Even the mines earned me a tidy profit...

And now, I was looking to settle. *Settle, where?* At the Mashton Fair, I saw this girl with wide expressive eyes of a bountiful blue... just like her father's...

... a father who looked like me...

(... with some variation, of course.)

A silent stillness etched within when I saw her, and I thought...

... give in...

... and take that handsome prize.

This one had charm...

... so I waited with baited breath.

I looked at her hands; no rings on fingers; no hopes to regret...

... and I dove in.

'How d'you do, miss?'

She turned to me, 'Sir?'

The lass was prettier than the freshest daisy; better than a mare in the field...

... she was... she was...

'I'm Jonah Ebenezer Hathaway,' I introduced myself. 'Your servant, miss.'

She blushed, 'I'm Amber Leigh Daye, and this is my brother Ross, and my Ma and Pa.'

I shook hands with them. 'Pleased to meet you all.'

I was still ogling in my mind and the eye within saw something rather succulent. The oddity that her father shared my resemblance had tinged me; *I couldn't understand why*, but no matter. Nature had its quirks and today's scientists were discovering new ones all the time.

I checked out the family, and found them like down-home country folk, which I reckoned they were. Despite the scruffy background, they sure smarted up for the fair, such as this.

I cleared my throat, then asked, 'Been out here long?'

Mr Daye replied, 'Oh, a good few many years... a good few... umm... before the War. We live at Xanadune, Bravada City.'

'Oh, yes, the windmill property. I was thinking of hitching that prize, but something suddenly came up to attract my interest elsewhere. At least you've done well for yourselves there, ' I smiled at them.

'Better than that,' Mr Daye boasted, 'The grain that comes from it feeds the Army at the Fort.'

'You don't say,' I found my match here, in shrewdness. 'Seems I've got a line of competition. Where do you work?'

'Up at the mines.'

'Yeah?' Oh, boy, this was bigger than I thought... I feared he would be a bit of a bigwig and, *oh dear, there goes my game!*

'It's a gold mine. We get a small share of it as a bonus, if we put enough hours in,' Mr Daye said.

'Good for you,' I cooed.

'You've done well, too.'

'I guess I can say I had. The railroad was my business, I invested much into it, as well as other enterprises. Got me a fine share too. I'm looking into other 'vestments that I'd like to cover myself up with.'

I stared at Amber Leigh, who now in my mind, I'd decided to refer to as 'Amby'.

The father noticed this and tensed up. He saw how my eyes were touching the presence like a moth to a flame...

... *ever so delicate...*

... *ever so challenging...*

... until you get burned...

... *either that or you dealt with the father...*

... and the differences between them were nil.

'You've been eyeing my daughter,' the father observed.

I broke the icy tone. 'She's pretty, ain't she?'

Silence...

'Uncommitted...,' I droned on.

Amby was flattered with the attention. 'I've been working at home all this time. Never got with a man; not someone like you.'

I smelt an opportunity sweeter than the jingle of coins. 'Maybe now you should start thinking about... ummm, how old are you anyway?'

'Sixteen, Mr Hathaway.'

'Call me Joni.'

The young Daye girl smiled. Her old man took me aside. 'You be careful with my little girl, y'hear? Don't want no funny business or trouble. She is clean and pure and that's just the way I like it.'

I folded my arms in challenge. 'And you were such a pretty picture under *your* bonnet, Mr Daye? Come, come, I am sure you and your wife must have had court hops in your time.'

He flew off the handle, but for second. 'That is none of your damn... oh Christ, I am terribly sorry. I should've minded my manners.'

I went unscathed at the aborted wrath. 'No offence taken. You care very much for Amby here, and I sense she is someone worthy of it.'

'To you? Eh, you're just a flyboy with money,' he snapped.

'Don't be so dismissive. It may take a long time before someone plucks that sweet rose from your garden, and takes her away from you... or it might be sooner than you think.'

We stood staring at one another, as if in a shoot-out at each end of town. Naturally, I let my mouth do the shooting. I did not believe in guns, though I kept one handy on my person...

... just in case.

'Look, I see you are a very caring father, with love and respect,' I assured.

'Well, I do my best, Joni,' Mr Daye winked. 'You two go on and get something to drink. There's that new branch of the Farr-Out saloon you can head into.'

'Be my pleasure, Mr Daye,' I said.

'Call me Amber.'

'The Elder Amber,' I kidded.

I threw a bottle at the moon and was keenly determined to plough my shares into that Irish hole, standing there in front of me. I extended my hand and Amby took it, and we walked to the saloon.

The family waved us goodbye, when Mrs Daye commented, 'There's a nice looking couple.'

To which Mr Daye responded, 'I'll sees it when I believes it.'

At the saloon, we sat at a table and I ordered some drinks.

'I don't bite, you know,' I promised.

'Yeah, I know. It's just I've never had this experience before. A man... oooh!'

'Nah, it is nothing, just ease into it. I'm just prime company to you now.'

'But later...,' Amby wondered.

'But nothing. You enjoy your drink.'

I sipped mine and continued to see the stillness around her. The tension was so sharp it cut into me, but I was not going to let that deter me from her. She was a nice girl too, from an obviously good clean-cut family...

... who cared about her.

Gosh, I never imagined anyone caring *that* much in this here wilderness!

'So tell me about yourself, Amby.'

'There not much to tell. I work at Xanadune, help Ma with cooking and cleaning. Ross does his share and Pa works at the mines.'

'Just like that, eh? Were you born hitched to a wagon?'

'They settled down before they birthed me.'

'Must have been hard on your father, then,' I giggled.

'Very funny! What about you? Where've you been at?'

'Here and there. My family's from New York. I was born when they moved out to these parts. Got working and went on from there.'

'Ah, so you're the wagon hitcher,' she laughed.

'You could say that, yes. Would you like to see more of the fair? I sure want to call on y'all later. Can I?'

She smiled. 'Is that an offer?'

'Could be,' I winked.

'Ummm... you wish to sup with us someday?'

'I'd take you up on that. Get you out more, see the lights and all.'

'Thought one goes to church for that.'

I sighed. 'There are more bright twinklers beyond those discussed in church.'

'Well, then let's go find my folks and let them in on your proposal.'

I went up to pay the bar tab and we went off to find the Dayes.

CHAPTER XV

Once we found her family, I made an arrangement with them to call later in the week...

... which I certainly did.

* * * * * *

Amby was getting ready for the evening, when she asked, 'D'you think this dress looks alright, Pa?'

'Looks fine to me, sweety,' the Elder Amber replied, sitting in a lounge chair, reading the paper. 'Don't know if it would suit Mr Vanduhbucks, though.'

'I think he will like it, and anyway, his name is Jonah Hathaway! Stop making a toss of him.'

'Well, he's probably used to high-class ladies, not country-folk like us. See here, he's making a shine upon you. That ain't normal for someone like him. Must be getting desperate.'

Amby harrumphed at her father and gave him a raspberry. He laughed at her and returned to his newspaper.

She ran to the kitchen. 'Ma, how do I look?'

'Like perfect country bait,' Mrs Daye complimented. 'Hope he likes that sort of thing... if he really is *that* keen on you, he'd be happy to see you in an apron and hair curlers.'

'MA!'

Amby ran upstairs and carried on fussing in front of a hall mirror. True, she was just 'country-folk' but she had a charm about her. Her golden hair was put up and shone after a good wash. Her dress was floral patterned and went down to her knees. She did not bother with face make-up, but she made sure the area was clean enough...

* * * * * *

The night air was fresh, with country smells permeating and blending with the outdoor scenery. I rambled with my horse down the lane toward Xanadune, after a few moment's brisk ride. The windmill was a bit of an eyesore to me; but if you were not used to it, that would be the case. It did bring out that rustic glamour, which was hard to find in a dense wilderness being transformed into a thriving settlement...

... and out here, anything was possible.

I breathed a sigh, I took in the view. Livestock was grazing, preening or sleeping. Organised patches of vegetation lay on the other side, obviously *away* from the animals. Fruit trees sprung vines of bounty and a compost heap stood at ease. There was a horse stable and the grain silo used for outbound purposes, as well as for the family.

I reached a hitching post, to which I tied the dear beast, and knocked on the brown wooden door.

A young boy answered.

I took off my hat. 'Why hello Ross. Is your sister ready?'

'She sure is,' he said, 'And she spent a lot of time preparing for your visit.'

'Had she now?' I walked in, and placed my hat on the entrance table. I looked around me. The place had appeal, for some, and it was plain simple living. It was not what I was used to, but if I wanted Amby, I would have to buckle down and put my preferences aside. The furnishings were cosy, with home-made curtains fluttering in the breeze from an open window. Everything was in its place and well-cared for.

Mr Daye approached and addressed me formally. 'Mr Hathaway, it is good of you to come. You remember my wife, Mrs Daye.'

She came out of the kitchen and greeted me. 'Hello.'

I bowed to kiss her hand. When I looked up, I saw a spitting image of a doll that appeared so ravishing, walking down the stairs, it put a dent in my mind...

... forever.

'My daughter, Amber Leigh,' Mr Daye announced.

I took the young girl's hand and kissed it.

'You look beautiful, my dear,' I said.

She paid no heed to the comment. 'Awh, it's just something I threw on. Ain't no big thing.'

Ross was astounded. 'Amber Leigh, you'd spent hours suiting yourself up. Heaven knows how much bath-time you spent.'

'Oh yeah,' she retorted in a challenge.

'Yeah,' Ross answered.

Both of them stuck their tongues out at each other, with the usual fruit-based sound accompaniment.

'Now now, children,' Mrs Daye reprimanded. 'This is not the way to behave in front of our guest. And you, Amber Leigh, should know better than to battle with your brother like that, and in front of a potential suitor!'

Amby felt sheepish within a short spell of formality. 'Sorry Ma; sorry, Mr Hathaway.'

I was confounded by the scene, but ignored it just the same. I enjoyed a taste of her spirit and sprightly spark. It was good for the moment, but if I wished to further my desires upon her, *she would have to change*.

After a delicious meal of chicken, fresh vegetables, jammy bread and a cake topped with cookie crumbs on the icing, we sat down in the living room for a chat. The two children excused themselves for clean-up chores. I then noticed another person with them... I realised he was an Indian fellow. It surprised me to see such a man so bred into domestication.

Mr Daye had seen my countenance and explained, 'That's our friend Whatho. We've been through a lot together and have been friends for some time. I was in charge of Indian relations, back at the Fort, and had done so successfully. One of their Chiefs gave me this pendant.'

He took the item off his neck and showed me. I was intrigued and admired the unusual side-story.

'Must be the reason why there'd been no Indian raids in the area recently,' I surmised.

Mr Daye smiled and nodded. 'Yes, I guess that must be the reason.'

The neck pendant was restored, pride and place around the neck, upon his chest.

I looked around and observed. 'I trust this took some time for you to set yourselves up like this.'

'It took some doing,' he said, 'With Whatho's help and Cindy's inventiveness.'

'Whatho?'

'That's the Indian's name.'

I laughed, 'Oh, yes. I forgot.' Then, Mr Daye told the story behind it.

'An English phrase passing for an Indian name? I confess it does have a ring to it,' I commented.

'His father thought so, too, that's why he named his kid Whatho. You may still call me Amber. My wife's called Cindy.'

'The Elder Amber,' I grinned at my repeated joke. 'I find it funny your daughter is an Amber and not your son.'

'She came first,' Amber replied. 'Ross is from Ambrossi, my middle name.'

'Ambrossi... ain't that Italian,' I wondered.

'Yes. Centuries ago, someone married into the family with that name. The Dayes originated from Oconnalow, County Cork, Ireland.'

'Ah.' I sat back. *What was I heading into?* A mixed-bred, now confirmed Irish family, with an Indian domestic... *wow. Stranger things have happened...*

... but I knew a good thing when I saw one...

... this family cared.

Cindy asked me, 'What do you do?'

'Railroads,' I answered. 'I've invested in them and it made me a mint. I put up that mint elsewhere for further investment opportunities.'

'Like what?'

'Business, land, mining. Whatever strikes the fancy.'

Amber turned to his wife and whispered. 'See, I told you he was a Vanduhbucks.'

I overheard the remark and interjected, 'Beg pardon?'

He blushed mountains torn down by logic. 'It was not meant to offend. I was trying to be discreet.'

I smiled, thinking about the silly label. 'Forgiven. It takes guts and knowledge to cook up something to call one.'

'We'll stick to Joni, if you please,' Amber begged.

Cindy continued the conversation. 'How long has your family been in America?'

'Since the last century,' I answered. 'Early on, before the Revolution.'

'Mine came over, oh,' Amber recalled, 'Near 1812 or so. I was born in Chicago.'

'Oh. We passed through there on the way West,' I remembered.

'Please excuse me,' Cindy got up. 'I'll go check in the kitchen.'

After she left, I got to spend more time with Amber. 'Your wife is such a mother-hen. I wonder where she'd plucked you from.'

Amber smiled, wandering down memory lane. 'I think it was I who plucked her out. She had a difficult start in life. She was raised badly by grandparents who did not know what they were doing, and she became a runaway. She hid among the Indians, until she met up with me. We travelled together and went through a lot.

'Shows your connections to the Indians, understandable. Reckon it was the hardship getting out here that forged you both.'

'Worse. I got shot at by those looking for Cindy, *after* she became my wife.'

My eyes widened. 'Really? Why were they looking for her?'

'As I said, reported runaway. The grandparents sicced a posse on us, who we drove off. Someone looked after me and her when I got shot. It was said that he sent the posse packing in another direction. It took a very long time for her to heal from her early experiences. Sometimes I wonder if that is why she works so hard and does everything in sight. I feel as though I live like a king... or someone like yourself.'

I was flattered... and more impressed. With good solid values, life-skills and love, *this family was worth getting into.*

Soon the children and Cindy entered the living room and I offered to take Amby outside so we could spend time together. Permission was granted, and Amby and I made our way toward the stars...

... for the sky boasted many twinklers that night.

CHAPTER XVI

We went out into the cool night air and sat upon the long porch swing on the veranda.

A disembodied snarling male voice filtered through the screen door. 'Be in by midnight!'

... and I reflected upon my earlier comment about the wife being the mother hen...

... then I realised *who* really was the mother hen.

I laughed it off and got closer to Amby. 'Sure's good here!'

'It is,' she agreed.

'You cooked up a mighty fine meal there. I can see how you became the peacemakers in the county.'

'Ma is a good cook and makes lovely jam. Pa gave some of it to the Indians...,' her voice trailed off…

… as I finished the sentence, '... and they were never heard from since.'

'Until they run out. Plenty more where that came from. We supply them in the meantime. Maybe she'll give them her recipe.'

I couldn't stop tittering about it. 'As a consignment for peace.'

I touched her hair with my lips and kissed the side of her head.

She swerved to me. 'It's like that, then?'

'I'm running a high fever of fancy to you and, with your permission, I'd like to return and we could go out together.'

'You mean courting?'

I was certain. 'Yep.'

'Ask my folks. I see no reason why not. I like your sophistication. It is so unlike the bumpkins that settle here. Looks like I will have to do some speculation.'

'Speculate away,' I cooed. 'You're just what I'm a-hitchin' for... with due respect, of course. I am a gentleman, you know.'

'Hopefully a gentle man. You're sweet in a weird way. Not many folk come here for courtin',' Amby said.

'Too bad. They's don't know what they's missin'.'

We kissed in a gingerly manner. The stars grew brighter, but not bright enough for others to invade our private moment together.

'There are some finely-bred twinklers out here tonight,' I observed, after the kiss.

'Can you read them? I mean, I know there's meaning in how they are arranged and all. There are signs under which one is born, aren't there?'

'They're called zodiacs, and yes, they are based on the patterns called constellations. If you look closely, you could see an animal, person or an object, like a bow and arrow, for the archer.'

'I don't know much about it, but the study seems fascinating,' she sighed.

'Well, I am no astronomer, just worldly-wise,' I smiled.

She laughed and held me. 'No one's taken such an interest in me before.'

'Hopefully, no one else will be, either. I hate pissing contests.'

'Pissing contents?'

'Other suitors, who may or may not be as keen as me, with whom I would compete, should you see anybody else.'

She understood.

'So when's the date?'

I turned to her. 'I'll set the date and arrange everything, with your folk's help. Someone will have to provide the reception and your mother...'

'... makes the best food, ever!'

'I'll let you know when I am good and ready. Meanwhile, you grow up some and stop fighting with your brother,' I ordered.

'But, that's the fun of country life.'

'If you intertwine with me, my Celtic knot, you will have to behave yourself and be a wife.'

I put my arm around her.

'I'm willing to wait for you, too.'

'Long time engaging, she replied.

'Yes... it will be very engaging.'

We remained outdoors for some time. The moon was bright, full and lit up the night like a powder keg...

... and her kissing lit up my night.

I checked my fob-watch; it was nearly time. 'Guess your folks want you in by now.'

'Wait,' she turned, but I had already walked toward my horse to unhitch and rode away. I waved to her, and she waved back...

... as I left her in the night...

... and I had a fistful of courting to do...

... which is what I intended upon my return.

* * * * * *

I turned to Amby for support and reassurance all though our courtship of many months...

... that soon became years, and upon an anecdote I heard one Sunday, I convinced myself (officially) to ask the dear lady in marriage...

... to which she replied, 'Sure, I'll marry ya, but it'll take a lot of doing to get used to me.'

'I think I could handle it,' I assured her.

And so it was set. It would be at Bravada Central Church, which united all elements of Christian worship (though if you were a purist, they catered to those needs on a separate basis).

A high-string'd voice accompanied the musical nuptials of the day. I had to thank God I found something more worthy than money.

The contract was written out and enacted, with all the usual clauses added in.

'Jonah Ebenezer Hathaway, do you take Amber Leigh Daye to be your lawful wedded wife, for as long as ye both shall live??'

'I do,' I affirmed.

'Amber Leigh Daye, do you take Jonah Ebenezer Hathaway to be your lawful wedded husband, for as long as ye both shall live?'

'I do,' she squealed.

What a pick-me-up.

'You best look after my little girl,' the Elder Amber growled at me, when I sat back down into the family's pew.

I promised I would, while I still pursued money...

... nothing was going to change that!

After the ceremony and the lovely banquet we indulged in, Amby and I spent our honeymoon exploring more of the wilderness and decided to camp out in it. We'd spent a week away, and it sure went by quick...

... but not without...

I rode on in a faith of my own making,
To breed my soil fair.
It was bigger than Vegas,
and the colours blended in, just there.

Amby and I lived, for the time being, in a small apartment in town, near my office. It was spartan at best, but we were only getting started. I was too busy with business dealings to worry about it, and Amby did a bit of secretarial work for me. Overall, the marriage was off to a happy start, and we were ready for a long future together.

* * * * * *

On a wintry, discontented day of 1878, during a visit to my now-in-laws, the Dayes, I came across a small happenstance. It was an old wrapper which, I thought, was from a bar of soap or some bathing product, being used as a doily underneath a vase.

I was mystified as to why use an old wrapper, when Mrs Daye was clever enough to make her own doily.

I asked Amby about it. 'What's with this?'

Amby looked closer. 'Oh, it's nothing. Probably a souvenir soap wrap Ma kept over the years.'

'It must have meant something to her to put it in such a place,' I commented.

It must have meant something...

... back in the day of an old courtship, maybe...

... of her own parents?

'Ask Ma. She'll entertain you with a spinning thread over it,' Amby suggested.

'I do not mean to cause upset, but may I inspect the wrapper, Mrs Hathaway?'

'Yeah, don't see why not,' she replied.

She took the wrapper from under the vase and gave it to me. It had an exquisite floral design upon it, with the words, *Bath Humbugs of Fullonum. Made in Totteringstate, England. By Appointment to...* I stopped reading.

Totteringstate... the name sounded familiar to me... *it was... it was...*

It was where that bitch colonist went to, after she stopped *our* Revolution! She married a Redcoat... my mind got further... the Redcoat was a Woodes-Hastings, who came from the family that began Totteringstate.

So... she married into the legacy that was Totteringstate!

Amby came up to me. 'So, what is so special about that wrapping?'

I eyed her fervently. 'This paper is the cause of all our Nation's early difficulties. This is responsible for the continuation of British rule here. This... this...' I soon began to shake the wrapper at her.

'Joni?'

'Oh God. Sorry. I lost myself.'

I had to sit down and have a good think, and a good chat with her.

'There was a Hathaway from New York, early on,' I began.

'An ancestor?'

'Right. His name was Jonas. He was of the cloth. A churchman. There was a wedding done by him for someone by the name of Woodes-Hastings, a member of the family who built Totteringstate. This Woodes-Hastings fellow was a British officer, a Redcoat, who married a colonist. This colonist was responsible for ending what would have been the beginning of a new Nation. She only quelled it for another thirty or so years!'

'So she stopped the idealism for a while. We still got there in the end and now our new Nation exists,' Amby said.

'No, no,' I droned on, then asked, 'May I keep the wrapper?'

'For now, or Ma will kill you if she sees it missing. Are you okay?'

'Yes. Got a pen and paper?'

'In the roll-top, probably, I'll have a look.'

She went over to the desk and found the implements I required. I wrote the information down on the paper and folded it into my pocket. I returned the holy wrapping and pen to her, and got up.

'I need to look into this further. You stay with your folks for now. I will come back, hopefully getting to the bottom of what's bothering me.'

'I hate to see you in such distress, Joni.' She gave me a hug. 'I love you, even if you are a cruel business-type.'

'Cruel in business only.' I kissed the top of her head.

One day in my office, I had a clerk check up on that Totteringstate location in England. He came up with its history and its recent goings on...

... in fact, the place was so riddled in debt and unless a bail-out was decided, a sell-out would be inevitable...

... by auction.

Oooh, this looked like a golden opportunity for...

... *me*.

I sniggered to myself, reading the documents he gave me. The actual residence was called Totteringstate Hall and the surrounding village was named likewise (without the Hall bit). There was a pig farm that started back in the medieval days and the family itself had roots going all the way back into Roman times, or even pre-history. Wow. *This place really had qualities any American would envy.*

It also turned out that the family itself hardly lived on the site anyway. Maybe someone, one of them or a relation, had kept it up all this time, but it was not enough...

... the bills were too high.

They also couldn't keep up the demand for their specialty soap, the *Bath Humbugs*. It would be most prudent for someone to take over...

... someone like me.

I enquired by telegraph of Totteringstate's fate. The reply in return gave an auction date of 20 September 1879...

... there was much preparation to do.

I sold much of my railroad stock, as well as my other interests. The auction included a pig farm, several good parcels of land, and the soap factory too, along with the Hall itself. It piqued my sensibilities to think that I could buy *them* out...

... lock, stock and barrel...

... riding my rodeo into that English countryside...

... and, by Jove, I was going to do it!

Time had passed and the auction suddenly came up...

... I was ready for the kill.

I sent messages to my contacts in London to keep and eye on it and to make certain I got the property by fair trial...

... whether it would be fair to others, was anyone's guess...

... I just had to have it.

No butt-smacking, whimpering colonist was going to gain the better of a Hathaway, for I shall buy *her* out!

Naturally, I would not make the auction itself, for a logistical nightmare awaited me. So, one of my agents, Cecil Wolfe, acted in my stead and updated me via telegraph of any changes...

... or challenges...

... to my impervious work.

'Don't act too soon, until it is too late for anyone,' I advised.

I couldn't wait to tell Amby about it. I expressed a vague interest to her when I saw that soap wrapper under the vase at her parent's house...

... but I didn't reveal my intentions...

... not yet, anyhow.

Now, if *I* owned the property of Totteringstate, it would be *me* as the invading party...

... and ruling one at that...

... an excellent justice for the beleaguered colonial.

There were a few others who expressed an interest in the purchase of Totteringstate, with all the trimmings; the most prominent of all being a businessman from San Francisco called Sherman Tankard-Jefferson. His interests lay in interior design and providing mattresses for the district...

... and beyond.

But this was personal to me, and I had to ensure that I was the victor, all in all...

... the stakes were too high...

... and justice would be served...

... nigh.

CHAPTER XVII

In a small office, I waited...

... telegraph at the ready...

... and so did my opponent, Mr Tankard-Jefferson.

Though the auction was in London, we put in our bids through the transatlantic cabling system and prayed it would work...

... of course, with infant technology such as this...

... *delays are inevitable.*

And so, the bidding wars had begun... it was us v. London. The highest amount was now cast at $1,200...

... and for such a pile like this one, it would have been the bargain of the century to snap up.

But alas, no such occurrence happened.

The Sherman Tank appeared with his bid at...

...*$1,500.*

I threw another bottle at the moon.

$2,000.

The Tank got bitter and tossed $3,000 to the cause.

I smiled, then smirked and besmirched him at...

...$5,000...

... any takers?

My complacency was cast aside, when the Tank had blurted up silly, all he had...

...$10,000.

I decided the nerve was rawer than the kill...

... there were no more takers in London...

... everyone gave up or was scared of the aggressive beast that would buy them out...

... the buy out became worse...

... *$20,000.*

The timing was tense. No takers. No Tankards either...

... and the gavel went down...

… the announcement made…

'... sold to the highest bidder... '

... *me*.

The Tank then shouted loudly, 'Awh, no matter. I'll buy up a peyton-full of English rubble and haul that ass here myself! Now how do you like *that*?!'

My normal reserve led to melted laughter. 'Hope you've got the haulage fees covered, sir.'

I burst out laughing, when Mr Tankard-Jefferson walked out of the office in a huff...

... to get back to the Bay...

... and search for the precious gold that was English rubble...

... oh, excuse me...

... *masonry.*

Yet, I took the greatest prize of them all...

... *Totteringstate...*

... and all that went with it.

When I get there, though, I decided not to make any serious changes to the area. The village of the same name could remain as it was. I didn't care about them anyway; they have their self-municipality to content themselves with...

... *but in small places such as these, they will soon find out who their Master be...*

... *for I've got a nice spread of my own now...*

... and I had six months to make the voyage, and claim the property.

I went home and told Amby the good news.

'So we're going to live in England?'

'Yep. That's the size of it,' I said, 'We could live graciously and grow together as a family.'

'But I thought we moved all the way out here was to get away from the old colonial ways and means... now, it seems we're going straight into the heart of it,' she moaned.

'Well, it is... it was, for me. I've made some seriously good money and needed to invest it wisely. And why not an English property?'

'The English property responsible for those soaps and Ma's wrapper-turned-doily?'

'The very same,' I beamed.

She sighed heavy, putting her arms around me. 'Gotta tell the folks. They may not be too pleased with this.'

'You do that, but it is our decision in the end. We're married now. Maybe we could have some dinner and talk things over.'

'Okay. Sounds good.'

* * * * * *

After a lovely meal with the Dayes, we got down to business. Cindy was in the kitchen, cleaning up after the meal.

I was correct in thinking the Elder Amber would not be happy about us leaving. After all, I'd be taking his dearest away from him.

'We will miss you terribly. Gosh, you'd be nearly two continents away, if you consider this huge land, plus all that ocean between us and Europe. It'll be very sad for me,' he said. 'Ross already left for an outside job, and I'm left here with Whatho holding the fort.'

'I thought those days were over,' I joked.

He looked at me with kindly blue eyes and understood I meant no harm.

'They are, but this property is built like one. With Ross leaving the coup, God, we're having a time of it. Come to think of it, you splashed much dough on that old pile of rock back in England.'

'Yeah, so?'

'Well, Ireland is next door. You two could make a side pilgrimage to Oconnalow together.'

Oh boy, more family history... here we go...

He continued. 'There's an old legend about my family's origins. It started long ago with two lovers, Conna of Cobhayr and Lowry Cindihan (so derived from Cindered Hands, due to an injury suffered at birth).'

Amby asked, 'What happened?'

'It was said a malevolent spirit consumed the home (where Lowry was born), and left her hands somewhat wanting in appearance.'

He paused, allowing us to take it all in. It was difficult at the best of times and when it came to spirituality, I found it most impractical...

... for only money spoke to me.

Yet, I remained silent and let the old fella continue.

'When Lowry saw Conna, it was a brief, and done from a distance. They never spent time together... but there was some sparkle of a love interest between them anyway, though unexplained. Despite her being too young for him, Conna did not care and secretly pined for Lowry; the sparkle lay dormant, *but never died.* There were many years separation, and Conna had to prove himself, as he was about to be crowned King Muffyhuer, ruler of the Cobhayr district. To win the throne and the girl, he went through over three decades of trials and many battles...

'... suddenly, when coming through his final ordeal, a middle aged-woman came up to him. His reaction to this was joyful, and as he had no queen, he thought to make *her* one. He then realised it was Lowry Cindihan, his olden-time love. It felt like magic when they saw one another for the first time in many moons.'

I was getting fidgety. 'What does this have to do with the Dayes?'

'Let me tell you,' the Elder Amber spoke, 'After they reunited, they soon got married and Lowry became his Queen. During the private Act, they died and infused themselves into the earth.'

I couldn't believe such confoundedness. 'Are these real people, ancestors, or are you just telling a good yarn? It sounds too crazy to me.'

He was shocked at my reaction. 'Is it as crazy as your bid for Totteringstate?'

I stayed silent. *He got me there.*

He carried on, 'As a result, the Cobhayr District was renamed Oconnalow, as tribute to the earth-devoured lovers. It's a story I learned long ago, and we taught our children this story, so when they later make the pilgrimage, they know what they are a part of.'

Amby sounded blunt. 'Sounds like a fertility rite to me.'

'Not far from it. Just before they fused into the earth, Lowry screamed '*Oh Conna!*', and they disappeared without a trace. Shortly after, a newborn baby boy was found in the vicinity. A young lady, whose name was Daye, collected him from the spot to look after him. No one knew where the kid came from, nor did anyone know the whereabouts of the parents... *no one realised the Couple had fused with the earth.* Daye took on the burden of the child. The refrain of *Oh Conna!* whistled in the wind, so she named the newborn Conna Daye. It's a long standing tradition and I noticed you and Amby ain't pregnant yet.'

Amby shouted, 'PA! Give us a chance. We've been working in the meantime.'

'Dirty ol' coot,' I said to myself.

The Elder Amber defended his belief. 'Hey, I'm just advising you. All the Dayes, male and female with their spouses, since those early times had made pilgrimages and secured their rites there, until the recent departure of my parents for America.

'Then again, it was some time before me and Cindy had your Amby and Ross. There were difficult times in our day, so it was best to be settled proper. And now youse two are going away.'

I put my mouth where I wished I'd put my purse, like I normally did in awkward circumstances.

Amby gave her Pa a hug. 'We will be in touch, of course. We still love you.'

Cindy walked in at this point, all the dishes cleaned and excess food put away. 'How's tricks?'

The Elder Amber looked at his wife. 'Our daughter is leaving us. She and Joni are moving to England.'

'Wow. That's twice the distance from New York. Damn. Hope you've got a cable to write us with.'

'We will write to you,' I promised.

Cindy pressed on. 'Why England?'

I explained, 'I bought a house there... a mansion. Remember the *Bath Humbug* wrapper you use under the vase?'

Cindy recalled the moment fondly. 'Yes. We got it from a boarding place run by a French couple. They had these little soap things in the bathroom and this wrapper is a souvenir from that time. Amber and I so loved it. I remember that bath we took...'

The Elder Amber looked fiercely at his wife. 'Cindy!'

She giggled in return.

He exhaled sharply and said, 'Women... they just want to remember the sentimentalities.'

I laughed with him, and agreed.

Cindy continued, remembering the funny place name on the wrapper. 'So you are now the proud owner of Totteringstate?'

'That I am. Hardly anyone lives there, so I decided to have a go,' I replied.

'Was there a reason for this?'

I sighed and thought about my personal story regarding Jonas and the Woodes-Hastings marriage.

'I have a family story to share with you,' I stated.

'Oh? This should be riveting,' the Elder Amber sat up, eager as a child for a bedtime story.

I went into the past and shared with the Dayes my knowledge of the union, and how the Revolution was cut short by the colonist who married into the Totteringstate legacy.

Amby put her arm around me. 'So, what does that have to do with you, Joni?'

'That woman put her nose where it didn't belong. Now that I've got the power and money to back it, I could put my nose in *her* garden and that of her descendants.'

'Ah, a tit-for-tat measure,' Cindy surmised. 'I wanted to do something like that to my grandparents, but they were dealt with beyond my control.'

The Elder Amber wondered, 'How?'

'The Stranger who saved your life that time said that we would not have to worry about them anymore... it was left at that and I plum forgot about it all.'

'Maybe that's best,' Amber gave Cindy a kiss. 'You work too hard to give a penny to what other people think, and most folk in town here likes ya.'

Cindy spun around. 'Really? Gosh. I don't do much 'roun' here. Just keep things tidy, I suppose.'

I stepped in. 'Tidy is hardly the word for it, Mrs Daye.'

'It's Cindy, yeah? You're no stranger no more.'

'Ah yes... I need to remember that.'

We whiled the evening away, still talking and planning.

CHAPTER XVIII

During the six-month preparation, which I did not think would take the entire stretch, I spent as much time with the Dayes as I could, for Amby's sake. Her folks were getting on in years and it was doubtful *they* would just come over to visit...

... but if it were possible, you know I would do it.

We broke down our household of whatever essentials we had and sold most of it. What was not sold was salvaged or donated to charity. We even moved out and decided to live our last days in America at Xanadune. I enjoyed the company and convenience...

... no baggage...

... the new place was well furnished and stuffed with trinkets...

... which I planned to sell on, and stuff the place with my own.

I wound down my business affairs too, selling whatever shares, stock and interest in the various pies that baked within my financial life. While most of the money went into the purchase of Totteringstate, other monies from elsewhere came in handy. I soon began to search overseas business and foreign stock; I thought it wise to invest in things closer to my *new* home...

... and just because I'm leaving, don't mean I leave my old habits behind.

I also came across another property for sale, near Totteringstate. It was called Greystone Estate, which was owned by an up-and-comer like myself, only back in the 18th century...

... at the time of dear Jonas.

The monies I gathered from my other pots of speculation, I put in an offer for Greystone, in ready cash...

... and, after a time...

... *it was accepted.*

I wondered what I could do with another *peyton-full of rubble*, as Mr Tankard-Jefferson so sweetly termed it. Perhaps I could use it to benefit the community...

... a dance hall...

... an orphanage, with all the trimmings...

... or a school (co-ed would be best).

I reckoned it would be funny to think of attending a school in such an atmosphere of a rich heritage...

... *mine.*

Amby also prepared for her trip to her forever home. I felt very guilty to take her away from such a lovely family as hers...

... but we all had to grow up sometime...

... and she'll be a lady...

... *my lady.*

Her relationship with her family was extremely well bonded, forged with care and sentenced with love. It was most precious to witness, thinking I had no family of my own, with my people going, long before I stood well on my feet. I sensed the Elder Amber would protect his offspring as much as he could, and wanted to see me carry out the same...

'Guess I'll have to leave her to you, Joni,' then he warned, 'If anything happens to her, I'll be sure to fix ya!'

'Don't worry, Amber, I will look after, love, honour, cherish her. The obeying part is her job.'

He smiled at me, 'That's the ticket. It will be more than likely we'll never see you again, or your budding family.'

'You will hear from us,' I promised. 'If we could get photos done, we'll send them to you. They probably have places that cater to the need.'

'Just don't forget us. Remember the pilgrimage.'

'I don't think I need help with fertility rites,' I stated.

'It's the luck, rather than the rite itself, that counts. It guarantees offspring if you do it correctly,' he winked.

'You mean you do it *outdoors...* on the very earth that...,' I said dumbfounded.

The Elder Amber smiled. 'Yes… or you can do it in a nearby cave dedicated to Conna and Lowry, referred to as the *Temple of Oh-Conn-nahh*, for obvious reasons.'

'No doubt,' I sighed, 'Does Amby know about that?'

'She will.'

Another visit thus ensued, and we stayed for dinner.

Cindy came in after a round of stove watching. 'Hiya, didn't see you come in.'

'Cindy,' I greeted her warmly, after seeing the odd residue on her apron. 'Making dinner, I see.'

'Chops, homemade applesauce, a vegetable and rice mix, with a cream pie at the end.'

She smiled and walked away.

My mouth watered...

... again...

... what was it with this family and food?!

Her old man asked, 'Any jam?'

'With bread, yes.'

I piped up. 'Homemade bread?'

She glared at me. 'Duh!'

I laughed at her snide one word comment and suggested, 'Maybe you two could come with us?'

The Elder Amber looked at me. 'Oh no, not us. We're livin' fine right here. We'd be out of place in your English home. Even going to Ireland, where we all come from, would feel amiss. Maybe you could get your agent abroad to have someone rent the place out, and you could remain here with us.'

'No, I left instruction for Mr Wolfe that I'll be taking the joint over.'

'I doubt you put it like that,' he giggled.

Now, I gave him the *duh* look.

We gathered to the table, and ate another fine scrumptious meal. The women cleared the dishes away and cleaned them in the kitchen.

I called out, 'Amby?'

She was helping her mother when she emerged from the kitchen, 'Yes, Joni.'

'I sure hope you've honed your kitchen skills from the Master here, cos I want to eat like this when we move to Totteringstate.'

'It may be an imitation, but I'll try my best.'

She returned to her kitchen duties.

'You people have a very special girl here and I am grateful to know she is all mine,' I commented.

'I'm glad your match is complimentary,' the Elder Amber replied.

'Your loss is my gain.'

'Don't take her heart away from me, though,' he begged.

I saw the look of a man who was losing his daughter to a rich man about to embark on a monumental journey ahead.

'I do love her,' I repeated, 'And I will care for her every need, down to her pretty little toes.'

He gave me a disgusted look.

'Okay, I won't discuss the intimacy with you, then.'

With dinner out of the way, I went with Amby outside, like we did when courting. We did our usual run of star-gazing.

'I bet the stars are different in England,' she said.

'Don't know, my dear, but let us dwell on these beauties for now.'

We started to kiss and I noticed a flurry of curtain activity...

... the Elder Amber struck again.

Yet, I paid no mind to it, after all, we were married now. A father could do so much, but I really wondered about his love for her...

... was it more than a father-daughter thing?

I cared not to stay there and just enjoyed the moment of *our* intimacy.

Inside, the Elder Amber got close to his wife, and surrendered his moment. 'Let's leave them alone for now. They're alright as they are. It is quite natural for them to...'

Cindy beckoned his words with a kiss of her own...

... nearly catching up to us...

... at *their* age?

Amby and I got chatty and began a stroll around the bushes and windy paths of the garden. The fruits and vegetables were growing well and everything was full of life and wonder...

... *even on the inside.*

Amby asked, 'So when are we due to leave?'

'When my portions here are concluded. Oh, before I forget, I was meaning to tell you.'

'What?'

'I've bought another property,' I announced.

'Another pile of rubble? You need it like you need a hole in the head.'

'Amby, don't be dismissive. It's history at the best price; a cash sale. I've made good over the years and thought to spend it on something substantial. I could really put my stamp on it... on both places.'

'Can't get more substantial than buying another ancient family relic. What's this one called?'

'Greystone Estate.'

'Maybe if it's smaller than Totteringstate, we could live there and dispose of the other.'

'No, I want to live at Totteringstate. I have some ideas in mind for Greystone.'

'Suit yourself. I'll go along with whatever you decide.'

'Remember, we've got six months.'

* * * * * *

The next few weeks we started packing for the move to Europe. We didn't have much; just the basics and the fair whack I kept aside for the trip. It was a struggle to leave the good old West of America behind, after all, it was my home, too, but I felt so strongly that it was my duty to discredit that colonist of long ago and buy her out. It was a good form of justice, as she butted into American affairs, I would now butt into British affairs...

... just in the business sense, naturally.

It would be like a bone sticking out from the blade and I liked the sound of that...

... but I wouldn't cause trouble...

... I just wanted to make my presence known and felt in the country.

CHAPTER XIX

One late winter morning of 1880, our residency in America was up and it was time to make the voyage to the Old World. We were led down a path where separation would not result in reunion; it would be the last occasion my wife would be with her family. As I had no immediate family, my heart could run the distance, but I had to make it clear to Amby that a new life awaited and the Dayes would have to accept this...

... which they did...

... however reluctantly it seemed.

We said our goodbyes at the train station near Bravada City. It was a grievous feeling, having to leave everything I worked for and what Amby's family travelled toward. I felt we were taking a step backwards, but if I wanted to claim that property, we'd best get a move on. We packed light, as the journey itself would become an equal nuisance.

The Elder Amber could not quench the tears streaming from his eyes...

... right down his face...

... into the groove lines of his dimpled cheeks...

... especially into that scarry bit on the left.

To him, his only daughter leaving him was like a betrayal...

... a betrayal of solid hard work and sacred values...

... that travelled to the Western side of America.

But of course, like all ethereal things, work and value could travel *elsewhere...*

... and find a new home to breed in.

Truly, I could not see *how* he felt, but with the face he made, the grimace was too gut-wrenching to bear.

Amby hugged her father. 'I'll miss you, Pa. I know we won't see each other again, my heart and prayers are with you.'

'As are mine, my dearest child,' he said, still crying.

Cindy was rather composed for a person of her sex, yet the loss she felt was just as great.

'You take care, Amby... and you, Joni, you see that she's got it all, y'hear,' she warned.

I clasped Cindy's hand and kissed the fair matriarch. 'I will do that and more.'

The train soon pulled up into the station, as the steam overhead filled the air, engulfing it right down to the pores. The finality was as intense as Death itself.

'Too bad Ross isn't here to see to your departure,' the Elder Amber lamented. 'We'll have to write him and tell him about this.'

'Don't worry, Pa, I'm sure Ross is probably worrying about his own flock by now.'

By now... the Elder Amber reflected in thought. His sobbing became more intense.

'Jeez, if it means so much to you, I'd bring you along,' I offered.

Pride got the better of him. 'No. You two go on ahead. We'll be okay. It's our country now.'

'True,' I smiled. 'Maybe Ross will deliver some grandkids for you to play with.'

He grinned and took comfort in that.

The Dayes embraced in one last hug, with endless goodbyes lingering painfully within the train tracks. They broke up and Amby and I boarded the awaiting train.

We got our seats and found her parents still loitering around the station... *maybe for a change of mind?* I waved to them, as did Amby. The Dayes returned the wave.

The train huffed and puffed, with all its gilded strength away from the station and Eastward, chuff-chuffing away to itself...

... *as Amby caught a glimpse of her parents for the final time...*

... who were blissfully walking away now, toward their happy and established home of their Xanadune...

... in the Western semi-wilderness of America...

... while we were about to forge one in England.

* * * * * *

The trip took about two to three weeks overall; nearly a week to reach New York, where we boarded a packet steamer to take us to England. It was to dock at Sydmouth Harbour, not far from Totteringstate itself. It seemed like a small place compared to London, but considering we didn't need to go *that* far, Sydmouth proved to be more convenient for us.

The transatlantic crossing by ship took nearly two weeks. With the same technology that made the good ol' railroads, these steamers made a two to three month journey into a week and a bit...

... depending on wind direction, weather and other nautical necessities.

The ship was not a flashy sort. It was a practical passenger and cargo carrier. It had its stoking and belching steam up the funnel system, the people on board were reasonable and some were very kind to while away the hours with us. Amby took it in well. She looked forward to the exciting life I had planned for her.

While on board, I wired my agent, Mr Wolfe, to come meet us at Sydmouth.

About nine days later, at last we reached Sydmouth Harbour. A sudden storm spell delayed the liner by a few hours, but the crew made up for it, once the weather declared pacifist waters again. Sydmouth was like any other port city, just like New York, for instance. I sworn by New York, as it was where my family lived...

... but at least I wasn't born within such a rotting fruit of a place!

Sydmouth Harbour bustled with the activities usually associated with the arrival of a ship at port. I searched the area for Mr Wolfe, who would take us and show us around our new home...

... and it was handy that he had the keys to the joint.

A voice called out. 'Mr Hathaway?'

I turned to face a well-dressed gentleman in a semi-formal suit, top hat and elegant manners.

'Mr Wolfe... Cecil. You got my message,' I cried.

'Of course. It may be newfangled technology, but it made me get out of bed this morning to pick you up,' he said. 'But you've come a further distance than me.'

I had to agree. My wife soon emerged from the crowd.

She gave a shy and small curtsy. 'Mr Wolfe, I presume.'

'You presume correct. How did you know?'

'I heard your name being called out by my husband. Couldn't miss it.'

I held Amby and introduced her. 'Cecil, this is Amber Leigh Hathaway, my wife.'

'Your servant, Ma'am.' He bowed and kissed her hand.

'Thanks. It's really agreeable out here,' she observed.

'Agreeable, but different. Not unlike your Xanadune,' I replied.

Cecil looked quizzical. 'Xanadune?'

'That's where Amby was born and raised. It's a windmill property, with a small farm and some land attached to it,' I explained.

'Sounds dreamy,' Cecil mused, 'Well, we better get to the carriage that awaits you.'

We engaged upon the final leg of our journey, which did not take as long as the previous hauls. It was an open air type carriage too, so the claustrophobic feeling aboard that steamer was soon forgotten.

CHAPTER XX

The carriage journey took nearly a quarter of an hour, as the crow flies, so they say. It felt grand to take in the scenery around me, as Cecil and Amby held conversation together.

I let them get on with it, as I looked outside the window of my seat to see...

... cows...

... pigs...

... scores of sheep...

... farmland...

... in surrounding greenery...

... with spell of quietude that gave no answer.

I think I was in love with the place already, knowing I was just so close to getting there. It was a lot to take in, but considering what I ended up with, it was worth all the while...

... *at least the Sherman Tank didn't get this...*

... and I firmly believed he wouldn't have appreciated it anyway.

A short time later, an exquisitely classical building loomed in the distance...

... *wow*, was all I could say...

(... to myself, of course.)

Cecil pointed outward. 'That's your new home of Totteringstate.'

'Gosh, it's beautiful,' Amby purred.

'A peyton-full of English rubble,' I muttered.

Cecil couldn't believe what he'd heard. 'You're kidding, right?'

I smiled, continuing on, '... to an American eye.'

'Ah.' Cecil regained his composure.

Very soon, we entered the gateway and long passage inward.

Amby asked, 'Are the family still there?'

'Not living there no,' Cecil answered, 'But someone was in last week to brighten the place up for your arrival.'

I acknowledged the answer, as I saw Totteringstate Hall for the first time. It was a white symmetrically squared building, with many windows and decorative bits and pieces. The style boasted the neoclassical, and there was much greenery to compliment the comely appearance of the property.

It certainly came a long way from its (from what I heard) medieval origins. Britain also went through a classical phase, like America did in the past hundred years or so.

The property was in the middle of the countryside, where I'd wished to ride my rodeo in. It felt clean, fresh and without interference from other people or places...

... not bad for $20,000.

The carriage then stopped and we got out. Cecil beckoned us to enter the place, which we did...

... and the feeling of 'wow' had never stopped.

The interior was just as inviting as the outside. Portraits of the previous owners laced the walls, over the already brimming wallpaper. Various souvenirs from trips abroad decorated the inside landscape; bookshelves housed books and other various documents of familial business, including records of the pig farm and soap business.

I decided much had to change, and discussed the return of (at least) the portraits back to the Woodes-Hastings family with Cecil.

'I think they'd appreciate that,' he said with a grin. 'I'll have that arranged for you.'

'Their collections and books are also at their disposal (if not, for sale), but the business books I think I should keep, so I can go over their records and see what I can do with them,' I suggested.

'Yes, in time, you shall do that; meanwhile, you two need to settle in your new home. Off you go,' Cecil pushed on.

We spent about a week or so at Totteringstate, firmly holding the reins upon our new life...

... the pilgrimage to Oconnalow could wait...

... for now.

I later met with Cecil to inspect the other property I bought, Greystone. I had ideas for that place in mind.

'We could house a school,' I began.

'It could be one, yes. Singular or integrated?'

'We have both in America. I think co-ed might be suitable.'

And so it was that an interested party combined the nearby schools of St Netherwind for Boys and St Netherwynn for Girls, into one... simply called St Nether Wynnwidth...

... although in a few years' time, there was endless mischief between the sexes, resulting in the destruction of the former Greystone Estate...

... *when it burnt down.*

Thank Heavens no one was hurt in the damage, but much pride had been extinguished faster than the fire itself. I sucked my breath in, and took in the loss. In the end, I decided to sell on the businesses of pig farming and soap-making to a major player, in order to recoup myself.

And I made another suggestion to make up for the lost pardon...

... they could transfer the schools *abroad*, say New York, and keep them as separate entities, with integration on a limited basis...

... *and I would put up the funds for that, too.*

I blushed hard then, but wanted to be as philanthropic as my fellow Englishmen.

The offer was taken up and the schools went transatlantic...

... settling in nicely in their new home...

... within separate partitions.

I still had the Hall itself, which I was grateful for, and my keenness in the foreign market paid off. I also put up for auction some of the Woodes-Hastings paraphernalia in the household that the family didn't wish to keep. It was a success for me, as there was much local interest in the Woodes-Hastings clan, despite the family itself no longer being in residence.

Over the next few years, Amby and I soon had a growing family to run about Totteringstate. There was Jonah Ebenezer Hathaway, II; Richard Leigh Hathaway and my little princess, Cynthia Amber Hathaway. We went into Totteringstate village, which had a portrait studio (the latest thing), and got a family shot done of us to hang on the wall (with the other pompous oil portraits I planned), and made a copy to send to the Dayes, back at Xanadune.

An accompanying letter was sent therewith:

Dear Amber and Cindy,

We promised we'd write to you and inform you of our goings on.

Our trip here was long and splendid. We wandered through a wilderness, before we set sights on the glorious Hall of Totteringstate that is now our own. It is a beautiful and spacious building, done in the Neo-Classical style of the day. The house itself packs a thousand Christmases at once; it is of such grandeur.

We plan to make that pilgrimage to Oconnalow someday, though our rites have been already secured with three little Hathaways. There is Joni, Jr.; Richard Leigh and Cynthia Amber. Both boys are quite animated and their sister is a pretty little miss in her own right. We enclose a photograph of all of us for you to see and put on your mantelpiece.

Amby and I are just fine, and getting used to English life. It is not the very fast paced life I am used to, but this area is similar to Xanadune and I think Amby will come to like it here. She's already a good housewife and does much of the chores herself, with some help from the offspring. My business ventures are fair; doing well, but for a small setback on a property I purchased after my bid upon Totteringstate. It is of no matter and the issue resolved favourably.

We hope your lives haven't been too empty. You both have comfort in one another and your love is well shared between you. Give our regards to Ross, and I hope he visits you often.

Meanwhile, we are establishing ourselves well over here and look forward to hearing from you soon.

Joni and Amber Hathaway
xxxxxxxx

www.ingramcontent.com/pod-product-compliance
Lightning Source LLC
Chambersburg PA
CBHW030628190726
48286CB00008B/2440
9781916007024